It's All Shoes

A Collection of Essays, Poems & Stories About
Women and Their Unusual Relationship to Shoes

Edited by Pamela L. Laskin
Co-editors: Lyn Di Iorio and Karen Clark

Plain View Press, LLC   www. plainviewpress.net
1101 W. 34th Street, STE 404   Austin, TX 78705

ISBN: 978-1-63210-012-2
Library of Congress Control Number: 2015945783

Cover photo permission of Patty Nasty
Cover design by Pam Knight
Section photos by Joe Zarba

Acknowledgements
All essays by Pamela Laskin were previously published in *My Life In Shoes* (World Audience Press, Inc, 2011). "Shoes" by Phebus Etienne was previously published in *Callaloo* (Fall 2000).

.

 We Find Healing In Existing Reality
Plain View Press is a 36-year-old issue-based literary publishing house. Our books result from artistic collaboration between writers, artists, and editors. Over the years we have become a far-flung community of activists whose energies bring humanitarian enlightenment and hope to individuals and communities grappling with the major issues of our time—peace, justice, the environment, education and gender. This is a humane and highly creative group of people committed to art and social change. The poems, stories, essays, non-fiction explorations of major issues are significant evidence that despite the relentless violence of our time, there is hope and there is art to show the human face of it.

To all the women

whose shoes we have walked in

Contents

Introduction by Pamela Laskin

Shoe-mania is a hunger, a craving, with historical, mythological and cultural roots. In Hans Christian Andersen's beloved fairy-tale "The Red Shoes," a young girl is consumed by such a powerful desire that "she took the shoes from the shelf and fastened them on, feeling it would do no harm. But as soon as they touched her heels and toes, she was overcome with the urge to dance." These red shoes propel the girl to dance incessantly, until she begs an executioner to "cut off her shoes and free her from this horrid fate." With her feet cut off, she is now a cripple, while the red shoes, "kept on dancing through the forest and over the hill and out of sight." Clarissa Pinkola Estes, PhD, in her book, *Women Who Run With the Wolves,* addresses the archetypal symbolism of the shoe that goes back to ancient times, "when shoes were a mark of authority: rulers had them; slaves didn't." According to Estes, "In this tale, we see that the child loses the red shoes that she has fashioned for herself, those that have made her special, and rich in her own way. The handmade shoes are marks of her rising out of a mean, psychic existence into a life of her own design. Her shoes represent an enormous and literal step toward integration of her resourceful feminine nature in day-to-day life" (p. 238).

It's not just the shoes that carry a message, but the feet inside them. In ancient China, women had their feet bound in order to display small and terrifically feminine feet. This statement is inseparable from the metaphor of what resides in the deepest recesses of our inner psyches: who am I, if not for the shoes that I wear? Losing these red shoes that have made the young girl feel special represents a loss of the self, for indeed our shoes are a mark of our identity. Perhaps more significantly, women find, even more than their style of dress, that the shoes on their feet are a definition of the self.

It is not by accident that shoes figure heavily in fairy tales, for fairy tales articulate the fears, desires and impulses of the collective unconscious in a format that is easily understood by even the smallest child, but whose implications and subtleties are often not fully grasped until adulthood. Coupling the words "fairy tale" and "shoe" immediately brings several tales to mind. Cinderella—the shoe as identity, as a symbol of uniqueness, for *this* shoe can only fit *this* one perfect bride for *this* prince. Yet, the glass slipper serves a dual purpose, also symbolizing the folly of attempting to be what you are *not*—for Cinderella's stepsisters mutilate themselves in vain, trying to cram their feet into the dainty shoe. There are the Twelve Dancing Princesses, who nightly defy their father's wish to keep them locked in the metaphorical chastity belt that is his castle, slipping away instead to dance their shoes to rags by dawn. Here, the shoes serve as metaphors for the failure of patriarchal vigilance and repression to constrain burgeoning adolescent feminine sexuality.

Shoes have their darker side, as well. There is the story of the Shoemaker and the Elves, in which we learn that it does not do to pry too closely into the origins of mysterious blessings, lest they vanish away as swiftly as they came. Darkest of all, perhaps, is the judgment that overtakes Snow White's wicked stepmother—"Iron slippers had already been put upon the fire, and they were brought in with tongs, and set before her. Then she was forced to put on the red-hot shoes, and dance in them until she dropped down dead." Was this story, perhaps, the inspiration for the Andersen tale of "The Red Shoes" in which the shoes themselves, fiery-red as the iron shoes forced upon the reluctant feet of the wicked queen, punish their owner's vanity (the dominant character trait of Snow White's stepmother)? More significantly, the girl is also punished for her own stubborn self-expression, manifested by her insistence on choosing her own footwear. The shoes dance away with the girl, giving her no respite, until at last she begs for mercy and submits to having her feet cut off lest she, too, should dance herself to death. Here are two stern (and very frightening) warnings of what may befall a female who defies the powers that be.

Yet shoes continue to fascinate, to beguile, to draw women with an almost irresistible allure. When I first decided to compile an anthology about women and their relationship to shoes, I discussed this with my co-editor Lyn Di Iorio and with my female friends and colleagues, many of whom are writers. I was bowled over by the enthusiasm generated by this theme. Everyone had a shoe story: memories (good and bad) of their first Oxfords; of their first pair of Mary Janes; of forcing their feet into shoes too small, just for the sake of beauty; of those special prom shoes; of the treacherous fights between mothers and daughters over shoes, which made so much sense to me. If shoes are a mark of identity, it is evident that adolescence would generate new levels of division between mothers and daughters, who have different ideas of personal journeys. The daughter who chooses to set out on Frost's "road not taken" will also desire to walk that road in her own style of dressed feet.

The concept of "dressed feet" and the split between mothers and daughters addresses the theme that we all have "ghosts" in our shoe closet, and the shoes we select are often a by-product of the ghosts we are consumed by. My own mother was schizophrenic, and her shoeless ugly feet motivated my personal hunger to own dozens of different styled shoes. Shoes, like a fairy tale, possessed a certain kind of magic. Every female can connect to that moment when Dorothy adorns herself with the sparkled ruby-red slippers, clicks her heels together and chants, "There's no place like home. There's no place like home."

The book is divided into three parts: the Past, the Present, and the Future. Not surprisingly, some of the essays in Part I deal with shoes as they play out in either a struggle or a meeting of minds between a mother and her child. In "Stepping Out in Style," Juliet Howard recalls both the trauma and the ultimate triumph of coming out as a lesbian woman, announcing her sexuality to her mother by wearing traditionally masculine wing-tip shoes on her feet while her partner stands at her side. Lynn Dion recalls the ecstasy of a very private early-morning waltz on a frozen pond in a much longed-for pair of ice skates. Ourida Chaal, a French writer of Algerian descent, recollects the long-ago night that she lay awake waiting for the Social Services workers to remove her from her parents' home, wondering whether the only pair of battered shoes she owned would fit into the new life she was entering. Several of my own pieces evoke the anger and abandonment I felt as the child of a periodically institutionalized schizophrenic mother, and my attempts (never quite successful) to fit in, by finding fitting footwear that would make me acceptable to "normal" kids and their "normal" moms. And Suzanne Weyn's fictional tale, "March 15 Meets Chiron," throws a twist onto the Andersen tale of the red shoes. Weyn's heroine defiantly buys the longed-for red shoes, even as she recalls the humiliation of wearing a similar pair to her first communion and realizing, to her horror, that the white polish with which her mother had lacquered them was chipping off as she approached the communion rail. Unlike Andersen's ill-fated dancer, this girl's decision—that buying a pair of red shoes that make you feel like dancing is more important than spending your money for items on the grocery list—is rewarded by a joyous surge of self-esteem, and a feeling that she is now akin to the stars in the sky.

Feet understand that hunger for shoes that will guide us home—and beyond. Our lives may be challenging, our relationships may be sour, our bosses may be awful, our mothers may not love us, but that special pair of shoes can make us feel like queens on a throne. In Part II, women consider how their shoes function as an expression of their adult selves. Lisa Coico relates how, on a long-ago summer internship, she donned a pair of size 4 ½ boys' construction boots when she came to a fork in the road—marriage to a controlling boyfriend, or an academic career?—and let her boots choose the path that ultimately led to their wearer's becoming the current President of CUNY's City College. Mardi Jaskot's "Red Wing Work Boots" tell the world "I have a girl's body, but my soul is Tommy Lee Jones." Patty Nasey lets the shoe drop on the *other* side of shoe mania—a hilarious insider's look at what she refers to as *Shoes-a-palooza*, a cocktail-fueled extravaganza for designers and marketers of shoes, whose collective motto is "An addicted customer is the best customer." Diane Goettel recollects coming to sexual maturity with the advent of her first love and her first pair of high heels in "Sharps." Mary Morris reflects on a life of shoe-resistance triggered by her overly fashionable mother's obsession with being beautifully turned out at all times, and tells how her disregard of what she could put on her feet finally crumbled when the only thing on her foot was—a cast! And Lyn Di Iorio chronicles a lyrical love affair with the husband she first knew as a slightly annoying classmate, back when she was still dreaming of studying at a major university as a girl in a Puerto Rican parochial school. The red Clarks loafers she wore as she boarded the plane that would take her to Harvard are eventually joined in her closet by a pair of beautiful, fabulously expensive Moschino heels that pain her feet when the once-annoying classmate, now a handsome lawyer and her fiancé, squires her to a party attended by the elite of the Washington, D.C. legal world. The Moschino shoes retire to the back of the closet after the party, only to return for an unforgettable comeback at their wedding, over which Judge Sonia Sotomayer presides, as the author "dances into life" in her fairy-tale shoes.

In Part III—The Future—Mary Frankel reflects on a lifetime spent trying to combine a love of stylish shoes with coddling her bunions, and concludes that post-retirement Shoe Life is going no place but up. And in conclusion, I dream of a barefoot world, a world of getting back to basics, of contact with the earth—a world in which we discard false values and status symbol footwear, and become our essential selves.

Thomas Carlyle's *Sartor Resartus* (*The Tailor Retailored*) famously grapples with the question of whether a man's essential self is expressed by his mode of dress, or whether it is more accurate to say that the mode of dress is chosen to conceal the essential man. Had his wife, Jane Welsh

Carlyle, written a companion volume, she might well have called it *Sutor Recalceatus—The Shoemaker Reshod*. For it is plain to see, as we read the essays, memoirs, and poems assembled in this collection, that clothes may make the man, but a woman may look to her shoes as a means of either declaring or disguising her essential self, as well as her most secret wishes and desires. There is a language of the shoe, and in this anthology we have some of its most eloquent interpreters.

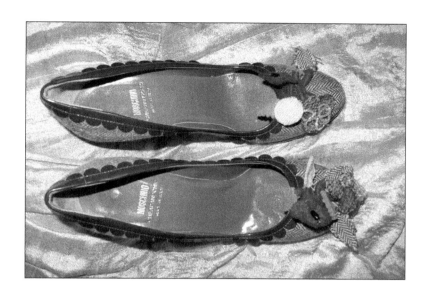

I. THE PAST

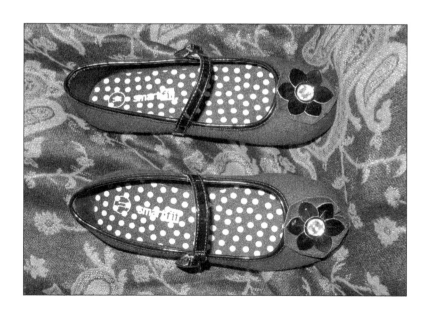

Dreams at the Tips of My Toes by Pamela Laskin

At night I undress my feet; they are ugly. No one has told me otherwise, including my husband and children, who love me dearly and extol my youthful looks. My unclothed feet have two hammer toes and both pinkies bear blisters white and round as the moon. They are not my mother's grotesque feet, but they remind me, nevertheless, that some part of her genes will remain with me forever, to love me or to haunt me.

In the middle of a stormy night, I am awakened by the hideous toenails that dress my mother's feet. They are curled over, a reminder that no one will cut these toe-nails; no one will go near them. In my nightmare, they grow fifty feet long, "Attack of the Fifty-Foot Woman" and they trap me in their cage. I attempt to claw my way out, but the vines growing between her toes, the rigor mortis, has grown a garden of rot. When I finally escape, I run like a marathon runner past the land, sky and sea. I am flying as if my feet own wings. These wings have taken me far away from the mental institution which houses my mother.

Back out of this nightmare, living my daily life, I come to understand the lesson I have learned from my mother's feet. She has lived with these feet for seventy plus years, and now they are still as statues. She is stuck inside the mental cage, whose thick bars grew locks long ago. Yet, there was one miraculous moment, before her mind collapsed, when she taught me how to walk. When I learned how to walk, I ran away from home as quickly as I could; my feet were fearless. And though they were as ugly as my mother's, I had dreams at the tip of my toes, and nothing could stop me!

A Mile in My Shoes by Melissa Connelly

I was fourteen, shopping all on my own when I purchased a pair of black sandals with long straps. The straps wrapped around the calves and tied just below the knees. I knew I'd be styling and proudly showed my parents. My mother, tactfully silent, managed a trace of a smile. My father burst forth with, "Who do you think you are, Cleopatra?"

"Shush." My mom nudged him.

I shrugged it off. I'd have to, if I were going to be a teenage trendsetter.

At least my father called me a queen. My brother looked at my feet and hissed, "Roman slave girl."

Undaunted, I forged ahead, but by the end of two days I felt like a slave girl. My calves were covered with welts and bruises. I tried tying them different ways, but nothing would relieve the pressure from the straps and it was impossible to wear them without the ties. A martyr to my own art, I stubbornly continued wearing them—my own version of a hair shirt.

Wouldn't it be nice if we could learn our lessons just once? But no, fashion life is real life. You have to learn your lessons from one painful blister to the next, over and over and over.

I'm awe-struck watching young people run down the street in flip-flops. The discrepancy between what their feet and mine can do makes it seem as if they're doing magic. I marvel at friends' ability to wear shoes I gave up years ago.

But that doesn't mean I stopped spending money on shoes—far from it. I have tried any number of shoes that people swore would work on my feet, only to be disappointed. Each time I have to grow up, all over again, reminding myself: *men's New Balance running shoes.* But like a search for the fountain of youth, I'll keep spending money trying. (Any suggestions out there?)

I still enjoy observing other women's shoes. I pay attention to the trends and have opinions even though I can't wear them. Red remains my favorite shoe color.

Sitting in the playground with a friend, we were discussing how you could tell working moms from stay-at-home moms. "Is it haircuts?" she asked.

"Sometimes," I said, "but you can always tell by the shoes. The working ones won't have raggedy old sneakers and whatever they're wearing will have a bit of extra style."

My experience has humbled me. I didn't have to walk in anyone else's shoes to gain empathy—only my own. But I can still make a snarky remark here or there, having learned it well in my Roman slave days.

"What about the at-home dads?" my friend asked.

"Oh, that's easy," I said. "The nerdy ones are wearing orange Crocs."

The Green Goddess by Pamela Laskin

I am six years old, and I long for a mother. It is true, I have one, but she is mentally ill and calls Creedmoor State her home. It is 1960, and though my official home is Queens, New York, my unofficial home is in Brooklyn in the projects on Pennsylvania Avenue, where being motherless is a commodity. I am more fortunate than some: I live with my Aunt Lil and cousins Ricky and Donna, four and six years old respectively. My Uncle Lindy lives there, too, but when he is around the screams are so loud, that the kitchen utensils vibrate. I am happy when he is gone, and I love this home, so that when my father comes to get me on the weekends, I don't want to go with him, though I grudgingly do. During the week he is too busy at work to have me live with him.

I often feel empty, as if there is a huge crater inside that has taken over my stomach, my small intestines, and my bowels. The only way to fill the hole is to abscond with Aunt Lil, and make her my mother. Ricky is too young, but Donna is my age; she can live motherless for awhile, and see what it feels like. I hate Donna for the privilege she was born with. I can't have her mother, but I can borrow her shoes. I settle on the green velvet loafers, size 12, even though I wear size thirteen. I squeeze my foot into them, a worthwhile endeavor, since they are beautiful: the outside is forest green velvet, and the inside, a lime green satin, with a simple gold buckle in the center. When I wear them, I am a green goddess, and I have a wide selection of mythological goddesses whom I can call, "Mother."

My aunt protests, "These are too fancy for school!" and I start to sob. The family does not know what to do with my tears, which are rampant. Aunt Lil relents. I have won the prize. Donna doesn't care. She will get two new pairs of shoes for giving me these.

I walk to school in my green goddess loafers. And even though they pinch my toes, even though they hurt my heels, I wear them, walking the mile to school and the mile back. I never share that my feet are blistered, that my toes are bleeding. I walk with a limp; I hobble to my after-school activities, never daring to take these shoes off—the velvet is too soft; the golden buckle shines. I walk these shoes to their demise, and am bereft when my aunt demands it's time to get new shoes. I don't want new shoes, not ever; nothing could replace this pain I've grown accustomed to walking with.

New Shoes by Anne Meara

Bad feet need them, good feet deserve them. That was the slogan for Julius Grossmann shoes.

We're sitting on the train, the Long Island Railroad, my mom and me. We're heading in to the city to outfit me for school. We'll go to Gimbels for a new coat, and then we'll go to Julius Grossmann Shoes, 39th Street and 5th Avenue, to get me the best. They didn't just have salesmen there, they had 'shoe specialists', who would just look at my feet and decide if they needed special correctional help.

I hoped that I needed special correctional help.

He wore a crisp white shirt and a perky bow tie. His name was Mr. Sandler, and I loved him.

He gently removed my old sneaker and held my foot in his hand. He told my mother how important it was for a child to have the right kind of shoe. "These are the expanding years, Mrs. Meara. You don't want to cramp the toes or the bones. You want the right support for the arch as well. The foot has to have room to grow."

My mother nodded and said, "She's very hard on her shoes, Mr. Sandler."

"Don't worry, that's normal, she's a growing girl." Mr. Sandler dipped into a shoe box that he had with him and pulled out an oxford lace-up. He handed it to my Mother and said, "Smell the leather."

"…oh, no, Mr. Sandler, I'd rather not." He held it under her nose. "Yes, it smells nice."

"Mrs. Meara, this is the best shoe-leather you can buy."

"Yes, yes, I'm sure it is."

"You see?" He bent the shoe easily. "See, not stiff, flexible. Let's try them on, darling—Anne, isn't it?"

Yes, Mr. Sandler.

"There! Walk over there, sweetheart. Does that feel good?"

Yes, they felt good, but they looked like "old lady" shoes.

"Does it support her arch?" asked my Mom.

"Absolutely," said Mr. Sandler, "and look, feel the space for the toes."

He wasn't lying, there was space for the toes.

Doesn't she know that she's embarrassing me? These shoes are ugly, and Mommy keeps telling Mr. Sandler how sturdy they look and how great they are.

She seemed happy and Mr. Sandler seemed happy. I was not happy. "Old lady" shoes, brown, lace-up "old lady" shoes.

That was in 1939.

Now I'm an old lady, and I wish I had my brown lace-up "old lady" shoes that looked sturdy.

I miss her.

Shoes, Cockroaches and I by Ourida Chaal

I live in the South of France, in a sleepy town, on the second floor of a high-rise block with my parents, who fled their native Algeria some 16 years earlier. It is 2nd January 1983; I am lying motionless in bed, pressed against a radiator, inside of which a multitude of dark, shining cockroaches execute an intricate, crazy limbo. I can hear their crisp, crackling sound much better now that my mother has finally exhausted herself shouting at my father. He must be down for the count, blessed as he is with poor hearing and his bloody rotgut for a faithful companion.

I cannot sleep, as a thousand thoughts riot in my head. In a few hours, my younger siblings and I will vacate this slum-like-home of seven years. I must not pack anything, for fear of unduly alarming my parents, who have been kept in the dark about our plans to leave. "Just act normal," I keep repeating to myself. "Social services know best."

But they do not know about my shoes, do they? I sigh, clutching my sheets. Now, unsettled, I toss and turn, briefly disturbing the cockroaches' orgy. "I should tell them I need new ones," I mumble, suffocating uncontrollable moans against my pillow. It sounds petty, at a time of emergency, to worry about a pair of old battered shoes. Tomorrow, I am starting a new life, in a beautiful house by the sea, but the only shoes I own both have holes in them. And I cannot bring myself to tell anyone that they make my feet bleed.

What will they think of me in this new place? Will they mock me? Will they point the finger at me? I have already polished the shoes—with vegetable oil, mind you—polish is too expensive.

My second-hand shoes have tales to tell. Their previous owner did not get enough mileage out them. But I did. I have walked miles in them, daily. I have skipped in them on the way to the school library (where I would stay until closing time, having convinced my mother that secondary schools required compulsory after-hours work. This translated as freedom to me, and my shoes knew it!) I have run at mercurial speed in them so I would not get caught by the security guard after stealing a chocolate bar because I was hungry. And, instructed by my mother, I have also tiptoed in them, while she ensnared my father in her bedroom, sneakily entering the room and delicately plunging a trembling hand inside the trouser pockets where he kept his money. I have learned, however, not to give her all the cash in one go; whenever I can, I hide a 50 franc note inside my shoes for rainy days.

Yes, my shoes have seen it all & have been with me through thick and thin: Accomplished accomplice, trained to deal with any situations. My shoes, I suddenly realize, are like me—criminal by necessity. But, despite it all, I believe I have a good soul, and so do my shoes. So what the hell am I scared of now?

I am slowly drifting in a peaceful slumber, while a trail of cockroaches offers my shoes their last saturnalia: it must be the smell of vegetable oil that sends them in a bacchanalian frenzy.

Red Shoes by Millie Falcaro

Like the opening scene in *Days of Heaven*, an elevated train traveled overhead against a blue sky—the same blue of my baby brother's blanket. He arrived in the cold month of March, and by this time, I thought he'd be returned to the cabbage patch where he sprouted.

The sidewalk, glinted with silver mica, sent a Morse code of dots and dashes along the path. I held onto my brother's carriage, as my mother told me I was going to start school soon. At five, I neither knew what *school* was, nor if it didn't happen within the same day, what *soon* really meant.

We were going shoe shopping, for what I remember was my first encounter with making a choice about something. Yes, I could put a Betsy Wetsy doll on a list to Santa, and somehow it would appear, wrapped up, under the Christmas tree. But this felt different; more like foraging for a meal.

The shoe store was small. The owner wore a plaid shirt, a clashing striped bow tie and a grey vest, and he smoked. His nicotine-stained fingers cupped an unfiltered cigarette; he nodded as we walked into the store. My brother began fussing, and my Mom rocked his carriage as the store owner asked me to place my foot on a flat black measuring device. After calculating the longitude and latitude of my small right foot, it was time for the selection process.

Here, the intersection of aesthetic and self-will first met. With one shoeless foot, I walked over to the shelves displaying the shoes. There they were, Mary Janes, with their classic T-strap, rounded toe box, and red leather. Not the showy red of the male cardinal but the reserved red of the mother bird. My Mom pointed to the same style in a navy blue version, and tried to convince me that they would have a more enduring function. I didn't know then that fighting my genetic instinct for the default blue would be my life's challenge. But on that day, my own version of ruby red shoes, wrapped in tissue and protected in their box, traveled home in my baby brother's stroller.

The Dreams Inside the Women's Shoes by Maryam Mortaz

Out of all the dreams that my grandmother interpreted for the women in our family, I liked the shoe dreams best. In summertime, Grandma would come to Tehran to stay with us, accompanied by two women. One of them was her daughter, my Aunt Ensi, who was a teacher and past the age of finding a good suitor. The other was my grandma's older sister, the childless Great-aunt Aziz who, to my widowed Grandma Khanum Khanuma's annoyance, always suffered from separation anxiety when she wasn't with her husband.

In a way, ours was a house without men. I seldom saw my physician father who only wore black leather shoes. And as for my younger brother, well, he simply didn't count yet.

I was shoeless in my dreams. Often I would wonder if these dreams were affected by my running around all day in my bare feet. At home, in the backyard, climbing up the apple tree and on top of the brick wall, I was always without shoes. Being a kid, I had no need to dream about shoes yet. This, at least, was what my grandma said to me, who refused to interpret children's dreams anyway. So, bare-footed, I would hang around the adults in the house, listening to their shoe dreams.

They would dream about lost, deformed, mismatched, broken-heeled, tight-fitting or loose pairs of shoes. They would analyze these shoe dreams, arguing and questioning amongst themselves for hours on end. These dreams spoke of their *bakht*, fortune, which more often than not had to do with their marriages and their men. Men like my mother's former husband, who, I heard, always used to wear glossy shoes and happened to have had a second life with another woman in another city while married to my mother. Or like my grandfather, who used to drink Smirnoff day and night, talk blasphemy and wear brown leather slippers until the last minute of his life. And then there was, of course, my Great-aunt Aziz's husband, Taqi, the bankrupt merchant with the pointed shoes, who had divorced his wife three times and would croon heart-wrenching songs for his incensed Azizeh below the stairway of their house.

I loved to hear these stories while the women laughed and roasted watermelon seeds. The roasting seeds made the same sound as when fireworks were set off throughout the city for the king's birthday or when someone in the kitchen was chopping onions for eggplant stew.

I'd often sit there on the red carpet, listening to the adults' long sighs as they crocheted bath sponge bags and table cloths. Their dreamless nights were a source of anxiety, as were nights when their dreams were too complicated. And so they took refuge in the poetry of Hafez, so that the great poet of Shiraz would at least help them interpret their wishes and their desires.

These women were believers in the power shoes had. For instance, if ever by chance one shoe ended up precariously balanced over another, they were convinced that someone in the family would be taking a trip soon. Us children would cheer then for the impending trip, while our Great-aunt Aziz, in throes of anxiety, would go around asking, "Who? Where? What is this trip that someone is going to be taking?"

Oftentimes, my Aunt Ensi would buy a pair of open-toed high-heel shoes so that she could unlock the severely closed knot of her fate. Of all her shoes, I liked her tea-rose-colored shoes the most. I also imagined that those shoes would be the key to her eventual suitor, a fair-skinned handsome man with a slight gap between his teeth.

And yet there were so many more beliefs centered on shoes. There was one, for instance, that had to do with rubbing the nose of the youngest child on the tip of a shoe in order to avoid the evil eye, especially that of a jealous neighbor. At these times my little sister, Mahtab, would cover her tiny freckled nose with her chubby fists and run away as fast as she could from Grandma. But Grandma would not give up. Holding one of her patent black shoes in one hand while still wearing the other shoe, she would speed-limp around the yard after Mahtab. It was an unbelievably hilarious scene. But even funnier was when Grandma tiptoed on her long bony feet, as quiet as a cat, to sprinkle a pinch of salt into the shoes of a tiresome guest who wouldn't leave the house after having eaten too much rice and kebab. Grandma's salt sprinkling took on special purpose when she went after Taqi's pointed shoes, every time this unwanted guest came to Tehran to pay a visit to his beloved Aziz.

I liked these superstitions. There was plenty of grown-up talk to eavesdrop on. My eavesdropping, of course, made my mother angry. She was tired of my dirty feet on her silk carpets; my endless curiosity also irritated her. I had too many questions: Why did she still keep her wedding shoes from her first marriage in a storage box in the basement but did not keep the shoes from her second marriage to our father? Why was she never pleased with *any* shoes? And how come Aunt Ensi, despite those pretty tea-rose shoes of hers, still couldn't attract the son of the chief executive banker who lived in the house across from us?

Why was I shoeless in my dreams?

I wanted to be interpreted. I wanted to interpret. I wanted to have a shoe dream.

My mother warned me that one day I would have huge feet. My feet would be wide and ugly, and no man would ever want to marry me. But my feet were still small, and actually fit into her seashell wedding shoes, hidden in the leather storage box full of mothball-scented folded fabrics of lamé, velvet, chiffon and crepe de chine.

It was a couple of years after the revolution that ended the Pahlavi Dynasty and brought the Islamic Republic when my feet really began to grow. This was during the Iran-Iraq war. By now, my mother's wedding shoes—one of them missing a pearl pin that made the pair seem like a one-eyed doll—did not fit me anymore. I was afraid. What if my curve-less body and undeveloped breasts, barely the size of small apricots, did not keep up with my ever growing feet?

No one had prepared me for the changes that came with adolescence. No one paid any attention to my feet, my swollen nose, my tender breasts and my moodiness. They were more concerned with announcements of coupons for the latest rations of sugar, rice, meat and soap. They talked politics and listened to war news coming out of the small black Sony transistor radio that was ubiquitously passed from the kitchen to the living room, and from the bedrooms to the basement where we hid during bombing raids. The wandering radio was usually turned to Radio Israel or the BBC, since local radio never told the truth about the number of casualties and the dead.

War, sanctions, the obligated *hejab* that women now had to wear, plus the execution of members of opposition groups and the hanging of that banker and his son who had lived across from us—these all invited terror into our uninterpreted summer dreams, especially now that my grandmother would not visit Tehran because of the war.

The adults had lost their dreams and, by and by, I found a new pair of shoes to care about.

They were the pair of navy blue Nikes that my friend Azadeh wore at school. The Nikes had been sent to her from abroad through the intermediary of an airplane crew, since there were no western clothes and shoes because of the war and the sanctions. I made everyone in the house crazy with my demands for the Nikes. My father, who was always on call duty during the years of the war, finally started yelling at me one night—how could I possibly have a desire for a stupid pair of shoes when people were being wounded and killed every day? He was right. Who really needed shoes when life was so short and perilous? Yet it wasn't so easy to smother the wishes of a fourteen year old girl. So I watched the days and months pass. I stood in front of the mirror and regarded myself. My feet had stopped growing at last, and my curves were finally visible. I concealed my hunger for good shoes and for a handsome man; instead, I fell into the world of books and I began to write poems.

After a long wait, I finally bought a pair of white tennis shoes from a heavy-set woman who lived at the end of our alley and sold second-hand western clothes. The day I went to buy my shoes she also made a cup of coffee and asked me to leave the last sip at the bottom of the cup so she could read my fortune. "Someone is going to get married," she said, showing me what was supposed to be the image of a shoe inside my cup. I didn't see anything there. The traces of coffee in the cup were more like a sandy desert road, instead of the picture of a marriage.

And rather than a wedding, we all ended up going to the funeral of Aunt Aziz's husband. I wore my tennis shoes. It was an odd thing to do at the Ma'sumeh Cemetery, as everybody else was clad entirely in black chadors and black shoes. Thankfully, Aunt Aziz didn't notice my tennis shoes at the funeral. She was too busy bent over the grave the whole time, while her narrow shoulders trembled uncontrollably like the tender, dry branches of a tree in a gust of wind. Even my grandma was crying that day. I wondered how many times in years past poor Aziz had reached over to make sure her husband's shoes were matched evenly and not thrown haphazardly one over the other; following her own superstitions, she had always been intent that neither husband nor wife would take their final trip from this world without the other. But now Taqi was on this journey by himself, his last trip to a dark grave that appeared more like a gigantic hollow shoe.

I was still mad at myself for spending my precious money on the faulty fortune-telling that the woman who had sold me the tennis shoes had given. But then, almost right after the funeral, Aunt Ensi came out with the news: On her way to school to teach, she had met a soldier ten years her junior; he was a tall, devout fellow with fair skin (but, unlike what I'd imagined, no gap teeth) who had immediately fallen in love with Ensi and proposed.

My mother screamed at her sister on the phone. She wasn't happy with the news. She said, "Is it so important to have a husband that you'd even accept some fanatic like this guy from Qom? Don't you know that all the people of Qom are zealots?"

The Islamic regime had unlocked Aunt Ensi's fortune at last, I thought.

Ensi was ecstatic. Eventually, two summers in a row she came to Tehran with Grandma to give birth to her children. We barely saw Ensi afterwards. Nor much of Grandma who was dedicating more and more of her life to her new grandsons now.

Tehran was under heavy bombardment during those last two years of the war. But we still didn't leave it. I got used to the war the same way I got used to my tennis shoes. The shoes were torn and raggedy by now, but I still did not want to throw them out. I felt comfortable in them. I would sit still in the basement during those red alert hours and watch my sister whose turn it was now to try on our mother's seashell wedding shoes.

I was fine with my own shoeless dreams, and in love with a seventeen year old boy who adored my stubby-toes that reminded him of cat's paws.

Foxie's Pond, December 1961 by Lynn Dion

The December I turned eleven, the big round pond on Old Man Volpe's land at the end of Maple Avenue, that everybody called "Foxie's Pond," was a mess. The ice was thick enough the week before Christmas to drive a small snowplow onto, and after the last wet snowfall Volpe had done just that. But the surface was scored and granular. It was no fun hacking over it on last year's dull blades, my growing toes bumping the ends of the hand-me-down skates and hurting in the cold without the wiggle room for enough woolen socks.

New skates were coming. The white box lay already under the Christmas tree. I was sure it was the one, and almost as sure that I could hear the keen blades lying in tissue, whispering my name with a voice of steel shaving frost.

Christmas came and went, and the new skates stayed in the box. The week was mild, hovering just above the freezing point, and the rutted pond wasn't worth a go. I sat at the window of my room under the eaves, fingering the edges of the blades and brooding.

Just before New Year's Eve, the soft weather topped out in a salt-smelling rain that swept across from the ocean and howled away inland, and then the mercury dripped like a stone. No child of New England needs a weatherman to tell him what that means. The promise of it settled in my belly, along with a secret plan that waked me repeatedly through the night.

The storm was over long before morning, and the blue-black hour before dawn was bitter cold and still. No time to eat or drink anything hot first—and besides, I might get caught and be told no, told I had to wait until the sun came up, and that would be too late.

I never wanted anything so much as I wanted that sunrise alone on the new ice.

An agony just to pee without any noise, no flushing—I'd hear about that later—and then to pull on four layers of sweaters, thick new socks, rubber boots and ski pants, then a scarf, mittens and the red stocking cap, sling the skates with the pungent rubber guards over one shoulder, ease open the kitchen door, and go.

The sky away east was lightening, faintly edged in dull red, and the driveway and the street were dry. The wind had blown the rain away before the temperature plunged, and there were no heavy icicles hanging. But every twig of the heavy maples lining the street downhill to the pond was sheerly glazed and beginning to glimmer in the first light. My nose was stinging already, and I pulled the tasseled end of the hat over it and breathed damp wool. The skates poked me insistently in the back through all the layers; they wanted the ice as badly as I did. I blew out clouds of breath to calm my stomach.

No cars. I hopped the low guardrail that ringed the pond, found the boulder I always sat on at the water's edge, pulled off the mittens and laced on the skates with great care. Not too tight, or my foot bones would ache terribly within minutes and force me to stop—and not too loose.

For my life, not too loose. I could just make out the transformed surface stretching away to the middle of the pond, utterly without mark or flaw after the rain, and I was enough of a skater to know this was no time for wobbling ankles. I packed the socks in the skate tops methodically with stinging fingertips, formed up the ankle lacings so there was no give, replaced the mittens, took a deep, chilling breath, and struck out fast across the dark mirror of ice.

I fell hard immediately, gloriously, and slid twenty feet in a semi-circle on my shoulder and side, the murderous toothed toe of one blade screeching behind me. It was some feat just to get up again—there was no traction at all, and nothing to hold onto. I rose finally, then began to inch toward a whole new way of gauging my weight and forward tilt against the cutting speed of the first properly sharpened blades I had ever owned.

I looked back and recognized the mark scored by the toe of the skate in a perfect arc like the wing of a bird, and I whooped and skidded crazily to cross over it. I fell again and again, but getting up was easier every time. The ice was so cold it was perfectly dry, and I wasn't soggy as usual across the seat and knees after the headlong tumbling and sliding.

The sun was coming up fast. I stood and gazed over the frozen expanse that was all mine. There was nothing there that wasn't mine, and meant for me. The morning itself was mine: only I had felt it coming and run out sleepless and empty to claim it. And the skill and desire to cut my mark into every inch of the glistening surface were mine too, and just being born.

I hit abruptly upon the exact interplay of weight, ice and blade just as the ice-coated trees ringing the pond on the south edge began to burn with red light, and I did not fall again, but began to fly. Sprays of ice shavings shot wildly up from the blades and sparkled everywhere. On a sudden impulse, I flipped around and discovered I could skate backwards, as I had never dared before on much safer ice, with big skimming crossovers that covered a score of feet, and then flipped back and went tearing around the perimeter, no one to stop me—for once in my life, no one in my way. The new blades slashed the way open as the old skates never could have. They felt like a ferocious animal part of me: talons that had always been there, unsheathed now for the first time. I howled and sang as the sun broke full over the edge and flung my solitary shadow across the ice.

I heard an answering shout behind me and turned to see a big man in a red sweater who came there often to skate, and who could do real figures. It seemed he had the same idea I did. He stood on the bank with his hands on his hips and his head thrown back, laughing when he saw what I had done to the ice. "Did you leave me any?" he roared. I glided in to the edge, sat on my rock and began laboriously untying my skates. The lacings were clumped and frozen solid in shavings.

"I'm hungry," I answered without looking up, and as I spoke the words I was suddenly ravenous. "I'm going home now." Skates off, I pulled on the boots and stood up, vaguely aware of a warm, spreading soreness in the big muscles of my legs. I turned and watched, shading my eyes, as the man sped to the very center and went into a beautiful spin in the sunlight, then I climbed back up between the maples toward home, the spray-covered skates nudging at my back.

Wingtips by D.L. Stein

He looks at the shoes. I look at the shoes. I want to look in his face, in his blue eyes. We both look at the shiny black shoes on the table between us. They have punched-down dots in designs on their tops. There's a name for that kind of design on a shoe, but I don't know it. I slide my eyes to the guard. His shoes: I imagine steel toes inside the smooth leather, aimed at someone's flesh. I try not to think it could be my father's. I look at my father's brown hands—no cuts or scrapes, just the short third finger, missing its first joint, that he's had for years. His nails are neat and shaped; do they give manicures in prison?

"Well, how are you," I ask. My voice sounds like it's being stretched over razor wire, almost a whisper through torn holes.

"I'm okay," he says. He looks at his hands. Does he have a hangnail I can't see? My left shoe starts to tap. I tell my foot to stay still, but it won't. I want to smash something, jump up, push over the table, level my Tommy gun at the entire room, grab my father's ironed prison work shirt and drag him out of here, over the dead guard's shoes pointing skyward.

"So, you take the dog to get here?" he asks.

"I just got my license," I say, blinking at the image of me astride Mike, his last hunting dog, urging Mike on with a willow branch that arcs near his nose, a hotdog speared at its end. My hand wipes a smile from my face: oh, he means the Greyhound bus.

"It's about time. Didn't I teach you when you were thirteen? What's your mother doing?"

What does he mean? She works at the shoe store every day. She says the women are nasty to her and the men feel sorry for her. She hates to work, like she's some princess who shouldn't have to. She's thirty-two and it's the first job she's ever had.

I don't say any of this; he might think I blame him.

"Well, is she dating? Does she go out at night?"

Is he asking about sex, I wonder. I still haven't looked at his face. With the tip of my finger, I nudge one shoe against the edge of its sole, moving it toward him. Maybe he knows I won't say, even though I think her decisions are stupid and she's lucky to have a job. I should probably do what she says, quit school and work too. But I have a plan; I want to go to college.

"You bought the shoes," he says.

Brought, buh-ROUGHT, I mentally correct, then wipe my sleeve across my mouth, like I actually said it out loud. His father made him go to work when he was nine. With any luck, I'll get to graduate from high school. I look down at the shoes my grandmother paid for. Saddle shoes, with pink soles. I'd wanted a pair for two years, and clean the white parts every night.

"Well, how are the boys doing?" he asks.

My eyes get a weird kind of pressure behind them. It makes me want to sneeze. Turning my head, I sneeze into my hand, then wipe it on my skirt. The guard hasn't moved. His gray pants have a crease from the knees to the tops of his shoes. I'd read that a man's slacks were supposed to break—that was the word, *break*—over the middle of his shoes. And his tailor should gently inquire if he dresses to the left or to the right. I can't figure out what that means.

"Are the boys doing okay?" he asks again.

My throat makes a noise and I sit up straighter. My skirt sticks to the plastic chair. I'm about to say no, they're not, what do you think? I take care of them after school every day, then make supper for us. Sometimes she comes home, and sometimes she doesn't. I lie when they ask, and say she's working late. They set fire to the field last week, locked the minister out of the house when he knocked at the door, and Johnny set Susie's bed on fire. I think Frankie still pees in his bed.

I shake my head yes. "They're okay," I choke back. "They miss you, we love you, when are you coming home, Dad?"

He reaches for the shoes. What's wrong with the shoes he has on? They're brown and shined, like some kind of hard wax has been poured over them. These black ones are dress-up shoes. Does he have to give them to someone, or sell them?

"Well thanks, kid. Tell your mother to bring the boys. I want to see them."

He stands. All the other chairs scrape as everyone in the large room stands. I stand up on my side of the table. I'm already an inch or so taller than he is.

"Too handsome for the devil," I heard my aunt say once. I was surprised when I understood she was talking about my father. Before he got the gold tooth. I guess it's his brown skin, blue eyes, and curly hair. I wave as he backs away holding the black shoes. He holds them like they're two animals he's got by their necks. The round braided laces dangle. All I can think of is rope, the kind used to hang people with.

Year of the Mary Janes by Pamela Laskin

It is 1960 and I have arrived: black patent Mary Janes. I am six years old and living in Queens, New York, in a garden apartment, in what Pete Seeger favorably calls, "Little Boxes on the Hillside." Though Pete Seeger did not echo these words until 1962, they had already been uttered by their originator, Malvina Reynolds. I am living in one of these boxes, where I think it is easy to hide, but I am wrong. The cracks in my life and the world are wide-open.

The world, too, has arrived. The first Catholic president of the United States has been elected. There is tension in Southeast Asia, between the north and south, ready to explode into one of the largest blunders of the decade: The Vietnam War. We are still living the Cold War with Russia, yet there is promise-with this young, handsome president and the Camelot aura he projects with his beautiful wife, Jackie, that great happenings are right around the corner.

My greatness resides right on my feet; shiny black patent leathers have replaced the cumbersome oxfords that were supposed to be "good for my arches." This never mattered; I would be pleased as punch to squeeze my toes into pointy platforms with no arch whatsoever, as long as they could look good. I was a chubby six year old impervious to dress, but utterly cognizant of dressed feet; shoes were my love object.

I go to a party in the spring wearing my brand new patent-leather prizes; they have a silver buckle so bright it is blinding. I am triumphant for one small moment in time, but when I walk into the room, I come to an abrupt halt: ten ravishing beauties, all wearing Stride-Rites on their feet. I had known Stride-Rite was the shoe of choice, but my father could not afford them, and he had assured me that these May's Department Store imitations were clones, but they weren't. I run out of the party crying.

Yet again, I am suffering the humiliation of the outsider: the only six year old in the universe with a mentally ill mother who danced in and out of institutions, and I had the bad shoes to prove it. Who did I think I was kidding? I could try to wear their wardrobe, but I could not wear their life; everyone could x-ray right through my charade. I throw the shoes into the trash bin, hoping that they'll burn.

The world begins to burn right before my very eyes: President Kennedy is assassinated; The Vietnam War is in full force and student protests start to accelerate. The idea of Camelot is quickly buried.

And I realize, hidden in my little box of an apartment, the one made of "ticky, tacky" where, "they all look just the same," that the exterior is only a drape; once the shroud is lifted, what's behind the curtain is nothing but an old wizard, rummaging through a bag of empty tricks.

Fur Coat and Shiny Black Pumps by Eden Novak

Ma had one fur coat, but it wasn't quite right. Either it was too short, or it wasn't the right kind of fur, or not enough fur, or maybe it just didn't make a big enough statement about her for the entire world to see. Whatever the reason, she needed a new fur. The question was, how to buy a new fur coat without spending any more money.

Where can I cut back for my Must Have?? Hmmm, we can cut out…. ah…hmm…food! Yeah! If I cut back for, let's see, six or, at the very most, nine months, I'll have it! Perfect.

So all six of us were put on a weight-loss plan, and Ma got her full-length Pavlis and Sons mink. It took nine months, not six. Not that Ma was counting.

There are a lot of attributes that I've inherited from my mother. I am not proud of many of them; one of the *least* dangerous is her Imelda Marcos-like, DSM IV textbook case of OCD shoe obsession. I love shoes. And Ma loved shoes. To Ma, it was all about what people—primarily, the women in our Greek Orthodox congregation—really noticed. Exteriors. Details. Those careful finishing touches, like ornate frosting flowers on a cake, or a well-manicured lawn and a fresh coat of paint on the siding of the house. Her closet was filled, not with glamorous designer dresses, but with coats and shoes. Pumps, in every conceivable color. All with high heels calculated to accentuate the line of her already shapely legs. Anyone looking at her was meant to get a picture perfect view, whether starting out at the top or at the bottom. *Ah, great hat! And that coat! But wait, look at the shoes! Or: Great shoes! Wow, those are some nice gams, but holy cow, look at that coat and hat!*

Now she had her new black mink fur from Pavlis and Sons in Chicago and a new pair of black patent pumps, all a perfect match for her gold Cadillac with the champagne leather interior.

And we were off to church to show it all off. The mink and the shoes, that is. She snapped when I asked if I could help her off with the fur once we got into the pew.

"I'm fine," she said, sharply but quietly, through the tell-tale Joker grin that always affixed itself to her face as soon as we stepped through the church doors.

"But Ma, it's hot in here." I was confused.

"I'M FINE!" she hissed through her teeth, still smiling at her audience in the other pews.

This was when I realized, looking over her shoulder and down the front of the coat she'd wrapped so elegantly around herself, that it was all she was wearing. Fur coat, ratty underwear, graying once-white slip, pantyhose with the holes in the crotch, but with nary a run down those elegant legs, and the shiny black pumps. I didn't need her to open the coat to know what I'd find underneath. That was what she'd had on when I'd seen her finishing her perfect make-up that morning.

Did she *forget* to dress? How does one walk out of the house without clothes on? In shiny black pumps, of course! And a fur coat.

Photo permission of Eden Novak.

Busting Out of My Buster Browns by Diana Raab, Ph.D.

My mother blamed her ugly feet, laden with bunions and hammer toes, on the pointy shoes worn in the 1940's and 1950's. So, the day I took my very first step she began to obsess about the type of shoes I wore. I vividly remember the afternoon when she sat me in the back seat of her white Valiant and drove me to the local Buster Brown store in Fresh Meadows, New York. In my little frilly dress, she lifted me onto the platform, six stairs up, to have my feet measured. I remember the measurements to be quite time-consuming and scientific, consisting of taking numerous measurements of different angles of my feet. The shoe salesman, dressed in a suit and tie, then fitted my laced shoes and then ran a mobile x-ray machine over them to make sure my toes lay flat. Looking back, I realize the seriousness and professionalism of his job.

From that day onwards and whenever I needed a new pair of shoes, particularly the week before the beginning of school, she drove me back to the Buster Brown shoe store for a fitting. At school, I was the only girl not permitted to wear slip-on shoes. The week before my sixth grade prom, which I was to attend with the cutest blonde boy in the grade, I told my mother I wanted my first pair of slip-ons. Against what she called her better judgment, she agreed, but I was permitted to only wear them on that day. Even though I appreciate my mother's gallant efforts, from that day on, I decided never again to wear laced shoes, except for sports, and became obsessed with slip-ons.

Today, we all know that bunions and hammer toes are more related to a family history than to the type of shoes worn. Now in my late fifties, I have to thank my mother's side of the family for my deformed toes and the bones growing in all different directions. I made the decision a long time ago not to become obsessed with wearing the right shoes. I wanted only beautiful shoes, because it did not matter; heredity would doom me. A few years ago, when we moved into a new house, we had to build extra shelves in my closet, to accommodate every style and color shoe. Thanks, Mom, for turning your obsession into my deep passion for shoes.

The Unsexiest Shoe by Laurel Kallen

When I was 18, I left Bennington College and hitch-hiked to San Francisco. My first month there, I saved up enough cash from babysitting and housecleaning to buy a pair of Earth Shoes.

Brown and chunky, with a squared-off toe, Earth Shoes, with their negative heels, were supposed to be good for your feet and body. Unfortunately, the price one paid for such ergonomic benefits was the compromise of a shapely leg. When my father, a Freudian psychiatrist, saw my shoes during a visit, he said, "They're ugly. They're unflattering." Peering at me over his bifocals, he did not realize that the Age of Aquarius was upon us.

Nor did my father fully appreciate the hippie movement's rejection of such ideals as the "lengthened and shapely" female leg. He did not understand that we hippie chicks were not supposed to worry about outer beauty at all. Rather, we had been trained to *get real*—to be *beautiful people*—i.e., beautiful *inside*.

In addition to the rule requiring that we be real, we had to follow other dictates. We could not set, tease, or color our hair. We were supposed to part our tresses in the middle and wear them loose. *A la rigueur*, we might be permitted two Pocahontas-style braids or, if blessed with curly hair, an Afro.

Body hair removal was also taboo. Hair was meant to grow wherever it did, so shaving legs or armpits could (and did) elicit stern criticism from our peers. We were forced to come up with health-related reasons for shaving—e.g., "My doctor says that armpit hair is an open invitation to bacteria and fungi," or, better yet, "My doctor says that my chakras need my skin to be hair-free in order to send forth their healing energy."

Either excuse would be met with: "Bummer! What's wrong with your doctor? That's really not cool. Maybe you ought to find a new one."

The use of makeup encountered the same resistance. We weren't permitted to wear any. Our generation eschewed artifice. In fact, going barefoot was the ideal solution to the footwear dilemma.

The second best solution was Earth Shoes. When I wore mine with bell-bottoms, the effect was tolerable. To Earth-Shoe my feet when I put on a dress, however, sent my self-esteem plummeting down the slopes of Mount Tamalpais. Why? Well, I was still a child of the 1950s. At age five, I had spent Sunday evenings enthralled by Shirley Temple's television broadcasts of fairy tales, with their Cinderellas and Prince Charmings. The expectations these tales nurtured in me were not as easily shed as a pair of shoes. So, at 18, when I put on my Earth Shoes and looked at my legs in the full-length mirror that I was not supposed to—but, nevertheless, did—compulsively consult, I saw my calves as short and stubby. I longed for "lengthened and shapely" Cinderella legs, and delicate glass slippers.

Despite an allegiance to my fellow flower children, I secretly wished for the 1920s, 30s, 40s, 50s, or 60s. Even flat-heeled GoGo Boots were infinitely more appealing and fun than Earth Shoes. After all, the Mod Squad birds wore them—and the leggy girls on the Yardley commercials that interrupted each episode—and *they* always had guys with British accents fawning over them—which brings me to the double-standard that governed our generation.

My disillusionment with the entire Earth Shoe phenomenon became complete when I noticed the hippie guys breaking all the rules they had set for us girls. "I have a major crush on Julia," said my buddy Jonathan, when a British model—the daughter of his parents' friends—stayed at their place in Marin County for two weeks. Julia emerged from the guest room wearing bright red lipstick, her fingernails and toenails equally dazzling, her hair dyed blonde. *Far out!* I couldn't help but think when I noticed her toes, with their red enamel polish, wiggling seductively in ruby-studded high-heeled sandals. I took one look at Jonathan's enamored face and knew what I had to do.

The next morning, I dropped off my Earth Shoes at a consignment shop and picked up a pair of silvery, rhinestoned spikes. I measured the heels when I got home. I put on ruby lipstick. They were 4" high. I put on my new Un-Earth Shoes, stood in front of the mirror and admired my long, shapely stems.

Shoes Like Barbie's by Gladys "Poppy" Perez-Bashier

At seven or eight years old, when I first started to seriously categorize shoes, I knew nothing of the history of high-heeled shoes, nor of their dating as far back as 3500 B.C.. I didn't know high heels were an Egyptian representation of the elite class—pieces of animal hide, held together by straps upon a platform of carved wood intended to convey a resemblance to the ankh, the cross with the loop at its pinnacle signifying *life*. All I knew was that high heels were a powerful extension of any gorgeous woman's life. My mom's high heels and gorgeousness were reserved for church on Sundays.

The other six days of the week, she joined us in wearing Earth Shoes. Earth Shoes were the sensible investment for a family of ten kids. Buy them slightly too big, and it took at least a year for your big toe to poke through the surface of the shoe. The thick sole would never, ever wear out and the heel design, which positioned the front of the foot higher than the back, was great for our posture, making it easy to comply with my mother's orders to "Stand up straight!" Although Earth Shoes were comfortably practical, they weren't pretty; I was never enthusiastic about a new pair. They looked like two bricks hanging off the ends of your legs.

By the time I was seven or eight years old, I had front row seats to three younger siblings as *real* babies. I knew that they didn't do much more than drool, cry, and poop. As the mommy of several baby dolls, I carried the roly-poly plastic creatures around the apartment, nonchalantly tucked under my right arm, but I didn't do much else with them. Who needed things that came with milk bottles no bigger than my longest finger, way too short to belong to any bona fide babies?

Enter the Happy Family. The Happy Family was the African American version of The Sunshine Family, dolls made by Mattel Toy Company. The Happy Family signified my promotion from fat, chubby-cheeked, life-sized baby dolls wearing booties to mature, skinny, boob-dolls in high heels.

The Happy Family was wonderful. It consisted of a dad, Hal; a mom, Hattie; and a baby, Hon. You might be thinking: *Well, there was certainly nothing realistic about adult dolls that were only 11 ½" tall.* But I would frequently pretend Hal and Hattie were kissing. Sometimes I'd find a corner or a closet to hide in, making sure none of the bigmouths could see me. I'd make Hal and Hattie stand face to face; then, I'd rub their hard bodies together so fast and for so long that my scalp would start to sweat, and I'd feel tingly, and ashamed of myself for making Hal and Hattie do that.

The shame, the problem, was Hattie wore mud colored plastic sandals, and Hal had plastic Earth Shoes…exactly what my mother wore. What I needed was what my older sister Juanita had—a Superstar Christie, a sort of Black Barbie doll in candy apple red lipstick and lemon-ice colored high-heeled sling-backs. After all, Ms. Russo, my second grade teacher with the blue-green eye-shadows, wore high heels that silenced the corridors of P.S.11 and made two-beat music as she marched us down to the lunchroom. And Charlie's Angels karate chopped, kicked butt, climbed fences, and chased down criminals in high heels. Cher's high heels made us not mind that Sonny couldn't carry a tune. I pictured Cinderella's glass slipper as a peep-toe high heel that Christie Brinkley would stride down the runway in.

Yes, it was confirmed over and over again: shoes that transform your walk into a strut make women beautiful. I, who loved pink things, dreamt of growing up to balance myself on three inch heels, arching my back and poking my ass out.

By the end of middle school, I was already 5'10". As a high school senior, I was 6'0". Since public school corridors are lined with a wicked artillery of tongues, "Tree" and "Giraffe" were bullets continually being shot at me. I spent my middle school and high school years towering above the boys, pressed as close to the wall as possible as I made my way to my next class, head bobbing above the other kids.

Because my feet matched my height, I shied away from celebrating my big-girl status with high heels. Even the pretty, pointy-toed flats were hard to find in size eleven. Whenever the shoe salesman was able to pull something from the oversized box that only vaguely resembled the display shoe, it would be in a width that had me praying that they'd stretch out as I wore them. Most shoe stores, especially the inexpensive ones, only cater to those *who haveth the foot of medium*.

In my teen years, there wasn't a ton of shoe buying, because there wasn't a ton of money. Summer jobs did occasionally treat me to fashionable footwear, but while the other young ladies wrote "shoes" on their shopping list, I jotted down "sneakers"—they were wider. In the 80's, a lot of the styles were unisex, and sneakers dominated the hood. High-top Converse, Pumas, Pony, British Knights, L.A. Gear, and Adidas "with fat shoe strings in them"—sneaks took me through the college years.

But at some point, I had to join the workforce and look "presentable." Now sneakers were unacceptable. I frequented the mainstream shoe stores, squeezing my feet into medium width shoes. After a bunionectomy on my right foot and a summer of wearing a cast, hobbling about with a cane, and swallowing prescription painkillers, I made it a point to shop at the superior quality shoe stores. Better quality means more money. I was thirty-two years old before I learned that comfortable feet are more valuable than money.

Now, I happily spend more money on shoes and I embrace my unique needs. But often, when I'm shopping, I still pick up the most shiny, fierce, kick-ass dominatrix heels in the store, enjoying the feel and the shape of them in my hands, before my heart sinks a little. Each time, I know that no one other than myself has ever told me that I was too tall to wear high heels. Each time, I wonder whether I'm going to hear myself asking, "Do you happen to have these in an eleven, wide width?" But then, the instant of hesitation I fear will seize the salesclerk's tongue—the ill-concealed pity for my bigfoot status that may leap into his eye at my question—makes me put them back down again.

White Go-Go Boots by Gloria Mindock

As long as I can remember, I have loved music and fashion. At a young age, it seemed like both went hand and hand. I must admit, I was influenced by what was happening in England. When the British Invasion hit, I was hooked. Oh my God, The Beatles, Dave Clark Five, the Mersey Beat sound…I was glued to the radio just to hear this music. Every night, I would plug in my earpiece to my lavender colored radio and listen to the music until the late hours. My mom and dad never knew that I was up until 3:00 AM in the morning listening to WLS in Chicago.

In the 1960's, I loved wearing mini-skirts, poor boy dresses, tinted granny glasses, fake hair, falls and the high pony tails. I would attach the hair to my own and instantly have long hair. It was great! When Go-Go boots came into the scene, I instantly remember telling my parents I wanted a pair. I loved wearing these white boots with my short mini-skirts and dresses. It was so much fun. Every month I would wait for the new issue of VOGUE to come out. I especially loved the fall issue, which is still their biggest issue, even today. I would copy the fashion. England was leading in the industry at this time. At least, this is what I believed.

I would wear textured tights or plain colored tights and it looked so cool with the boots. I had a bluish gray mini dress that I really loved wearing with the boots. My mom would hem my skirts up and my father would walk by and say, "That's too short." My mother didn't pay any attention to him and hemmed my skirts and dresses short. My mother was very cool and into fashion. She always looked so modern and hip. I was very lucky to have such "in" parents.

On TV, I would watch *American Bandstand*, *Soul Train*, and the *The Hulabaloo Show*. I knew every dance there was to do in the 1960's and I still remember them all to perfection. Even the Motown dances looked good in my Go-Go boots. I remember seeing the girls and their Go-Go boots doing the Go-Go. When Nancy Sinatra's song came out, "These Boots Are Made for Walkin," I never associated that song with Go-Go boots. There are those who do. I loved the song, though. I was a fan of *Shindig*, too, and faithfully watched that. I watched some of the girls up high dancing in cages. I loved it! I wanted to do this.

Another thing I did, to go with my Go-Go boots, was wear pale white or pink lipstick. Whenever I found Yardley make-up, I would buy it. I caked on my mascara and wore black eyeliner when I could. My parents did not want me wearing so much make-up.

I went to concerts, and always got to meet so many bands. I was such a teenybopper. I screamed during the concerts, but we all did in those days. A fond memory I have is seeing the Dave Clark Five, being in the first row, with my friend Carol, screaming "Denny!" Yes, my crush was on him and yes, he did wink at me! Me! I was so happy!!!

My Go-Go boots took me through a wonderful time, a wonderful era. I am so lucky to have been old enough to be a crazy kid loving her Go-Go boots and the great fashion. With all the boots we see out today and in all different styles, the Go-Go boots are still my favorite.

How well I remember going to a Go-Go! I wish I could boogaloo right out of here, with my hair cropped short, my white Go-Go Boots on, wearing my mini dress, screaming at guys in the bands, feeling a crush so strong for Paul McCartney (still have one). Live on, Go-Go boots and the 60's!

What a Steal! by Jacqueline Annette

In another life, as an undergraduate at a Brooklyn community college, I sold shoes. Years before, I'd dated a shoe salesman who worked at Saks Fifth Ave. He stole shoes neither of us could have afforded. I never asked him for these shoes, and was ambivalent about accepting such gifts. Who wants to think she only rates a gift that cost nothing? On the other hand, whenever I crossed my legs for maximum shoe exposure, I delighted in the envious looks and compliments from women who knew what my shoes *should* have cost, and the admiring glances from men. There's something about the elan of well-designed, well-constructed shoes. Shoes that enhance a woman's leg, create the sensuous tilt of her hips, give the extra height heels and platforms provide, and still allow for a graceful gait are to be prized. What woman does not crave the illusion of a longer leg? Since I was not asking for these "gifts," I never went to the store to try them on; yet, most of the time, they fit me perfectly. That was where the quality lay. Perhaps I told myself that, despite my acceptance of the goods, I was not colluding in his crime because I was never a direct participant. The upshot, however, was that I learned to tell the difference between the kind of shoes I usually bought, and the better quality.

Later, when I went to work in the Brooklyn department store, I knew the quality of a shoe was not only based on price. Sometimes it had more to do with the cut. In some cases, the materials were good, but the cut was poor, or the design was awkward and ungainly. Other times there could be perfection at a moderate price. I had a generous discount; there was no need to risk jail for what I could easily afford.

Our department display consisted of molded plastic feet which swung freely, suspended on a metal bar affixed to the wall, so that a customer could inspect the sole of a shoe for style and price without taking it down. We only put out one shoe in each color per style, and always the left shoe only, in size six. Specially ordered by a newly promoted buyer, the display replaced the free-standing units and tables, and gave the area the more open, inviting look that the buyer was sure would boost sales. The new display was the pride of the buyer, and he could often be seen fixing the selection. The shoes hung neatly, with the full color range per style, all going in the same direction.

One year we got in a line of shoes—*Elditas*, from Spain—with light tan wooden platforms topped by an array of color combinations and patterns. Bold, vivid, innovative designs on the wide wooden covered or natural platforms; laced up, sling back, or backless; moderate price; novel color combinations; and a comfortable fit. All this made them very popular with customers—and with thieves. There had always been a certain amount of theft, but these shoes brought out the thieves in droves.

There were single thieves; young neighborhood teens; couples; a slightly older man and women team. After a while "loss prevention" would circulate in our department, just to keep an eye on them. Some thieves would hide the shoes up the sleeve of a winter coat. Others would merely put their old, worn-out shoes into the boxes, stack them neatly, place them under the chair, and walk out wearing the new shoes. If a couple arrived, she would distract; he would steal. She would ask for several pairs in rapid succession; during the back and forth, he could skulk away with a pair. Sometimes they did not walk in together—he came into the department asking for a different pair for a wife or girlfriend. Either way, he walked off with the shoes while she lingered to argue about colors she, we knew, was never going to buy.

Most infamous of all were the "Size Six Thieves," as we had come to call a group of six or seven agile, pint-sized girls, all of whom wore size six. They shopped together; they stole together. They would order several styles, all in the same size and take turns trying them on. They tied up lots of merchandise, none of which would they relinquish while they made their selections.

Once that became too obvious, too risky, they shifted mode. Sometimes, while one was actually buying a pair, the others would steal. The size of the group fluctuated; often it shrank to a duo or trio. When some of them got busted trying to steal an entire pair, the tactic shifted again. While one of ours was busy waiting on one of theirs, another would casually steal display shoes. At first, we were only semi-vigilant. As long as there were two shoes left in the box after they were gone, we considered we had retained another pair to sell later. But later, the buyer would notice that shoes were missing from the display. Rather than breaking up another pair, we would put out the right shoe that matched the one that had been stolen. A day later, the right would join the left.

At that rate the "Size Six Thieves" depleted the size before we could sell them. The buyer, who by now was livid, devised a plan to stem the flow. Determined to have the shoes displayed, not stolen, he put out random sizes; if the left had been a size six, he would replace it with a size eight right. In their haste to obtain the match unobserved, the "Size Sixers" did not notice the size difference. At this point they were no longer trying anything on. They were simply collecting the entire color range.

This went on for about two weeks, until the afternoon the buyer was standing in the department eyeing the group of girls with open hostility, braced to catch at least one of them stealing, for as they roamed the department, each one seemed to be carrying a shopping bag of one size or another. By now, everyone knew them, so stealing had become more difficult.

Observing the buyer hovering near the displays, they had a few choice words for him. "You think you're so damned smart," they taunted him.

Suddenly, as if on cue, they produced an assortment of shoes from previous trips to the department from their bags and hurled them at him. As he dodged the rainbow torrent of platforms, peals of laughter erupted as the Size Sixers dashed down the escalator.

In the middle of the crowded shoe department, shocked customers gaping at him, the buyer stood unhurt, but shaken, a pile of near-misses in the form of mismatched clunky platforms scattered at his feet.

I understood it all. I understood keenly what it is about the lure of innovative, unusual styles that sets a woman apart, gives her an edge— the yen that makes some people willing to steal, to risk arrest, just to have them on their feet. I knew only too well that shoes can be a fashion friend to those with flawed figures. I understood how shoes could visually elevate not only the wearer, but her outfit. Accessories, of which shoes are the major and most expensive part, make the difference between a mundane dress, and an audacious appearance.

I understood the Size Six Thieves. They had more nerve than I would ever have had, but we were kin. I also understood their frustration. All that work for nothing!

42nd Street by Margarette Gulinello

I was raised in Harlem, in the eighties. My favorite person in the whole world was my grandmother who died at forty-six when I was eight. My mother and grandma were fun women; we laughed, played, and dressed with the care a scientist might give to concocting a new antidote. To both of them, I could do no wrong.

When Grandma died, part of my mother disappeared. There was an empty hole inside of me. Watching my mother be so sad was almost as hurtful as losing Grandma. I hated that I couldn't control my pain, her sadness or the simple fact that my grandma wasn't here with us forever.

My mother fell hard into depression, and I went from being a cheerful part of her to being an obstacle that was hard to deny. I had no father; our home life was rapidly deteriorating, along with my sense of self. Being a child who felt lost, and who desperately wanted my mother to be my grandmother, was overwhelming. Her eyes, dull from sadness, would gaze into the distance when I tried so hard to get her to really see me.

I would imagine I'd disappear and pop into a world where people laughed, had plenty of food, lived forever, and music was the center of the town. I named this world "Music Town," and I would be there someday.

My first introduction to dance was in junior high. By then my mother was a full mess; we barely had food, let alone clothes. She was self-medicating with drugs and alcohol at a frightening rate. My only pair of sneakers was so worn; I had blisters from the cold and calluses from the heat. I felt completely helpless and doomed.

We had to purchase ballet slippers for the class. Wow, ballet slippers. Those were last seen on our black and white television, when Grandma and I watched ballerinas in *The Nutcracker*.

"I'm going to do that one day, Grandma!"

"What?"

"Be a ballerina. I bet you would like that huh?"

"I would like—no, *love*—anything you do, sweetheart."

I couldn't believe I would have a pair myself. I would be the ballet version of Cinderella!

Whether I got the slippers or not didn't matter much to my mother. But those ballet slippers meant the world to me. And I would make her and my grandma proud. Socks substituted for the slippers for months before I saved up enough to get a used pair. Birthday money from relatives and running errands for the neighbors helped me start to save a little. When you're under fourteen, the money comes in slowly.

When I got them, they were barely worn; the ribbons were slightly wrinkled, but I would iron those.

I couldn't get enough of dance. I would practice to the radio in the bedroom. Most of all I would imitate the dancers I watched on television. As I looked at them, I saw my face, my body, and my moves on the screen.

I went on to dance for years, acquired several scholarships, and even attended The School for the Performing Arts. I was a dance major, of course. By then I was an official ballerina.

My mother was not getting any better. The harder I tried for her attention, the faster she retreated. I became so angry with her.

"Why did you even keep me after Grandma died? This life is horrible; do you even love me?"

I would just get a blank stare in response. The compliments from other dancers and instructors started to wear off and get old with me. Dance became something I couldn't use to fix my mother. But if I *became* her, she might want me then. I started drinking, smoking and taking up "new friends." Some "official ballerina" I was. Ballerina by day, slowly getting eaten up by the streets of Harlem by night. I measured my happiness against those I met in the street and those I met in the dance studio. Between the two extremes, I became the girl who didn't fit anywhere.

I eventually lost my dance abilities and gained a horrible grudge against my mother. I desperately wanted to be noticed. If my mother could just tell me she was proud of me for how hard I worked, and that she was sorry for costing me the only thing I loved! This obsession grew into every area of my life; I wanted to be noticed by everyone, and with a vengeance. Working part time to put myself through college infuriated me. But by the time I was in my early twenties, I saw a career opportunity I would not have imagined.

I traded in my slippers for black boots when I joined the Police Academy. Within two years of joining, I was an established cop, with a badge, a gun, and a pension plan. I even got a night off, once in a while. And on one of those rare nights off, I went to see *42nd Street*. As I watched, the magic came over me again. I must have cried at least three times; during happy scenes, at that! I wanted to be on that stage. I wanted to be that heroine who grew up in New York and became a star.

I started reading the trades again. A couple of months later, I read that they were casting for the chorus of *42nd Street*.

I am sitting in split position, in a room with about one hundred girls, stretching their arms. No laughter or talking. The smell of ballet slippers and new tights relaxes me a bit. My cousin Candace is with me for support. I would never attempt to pull this off alone. We are leaning up against a wall watching everyone.

"This is so exciting!"

"I'm not excited anymore—now, I'm just plain nervous."

"Why? You have the look, you can dance, and you have done this for years."

"I don't know, these girls look like they really know what they are doing. I hope ballet is first. What did you think about my singing when I practiced the song yesterday?"

"Well, if you let the nerves go, you would sound better. It wasn't bad, though."

"Oh God, I'm done, we should just leave." I realize I have been reaching toward my toes; my thighs are numb, and I stand up.

"Don't leave now, you have nothing to lose. I'll be here, rooting you on. Stop being nervous—you're a cop, for crying out loud!"

"Shhhh...I wrote I'm unemployed on the form! I'd be utterly embarrassed if they knew that! And on top of it, what if I stink? Imagine, they'd tell me to keep my day job!"

Candace laughs. A few girls walk in, look for the sign-in sheet, and I must have looked at my watch a hundred times. The smell of my ballet shoes reassures me I am just as good as the other dancers. The ribbons are soft and hug my calves perfectly.

I was in LaGuardia School of Performing Arts; a dance major. I loved being able to say that out loud. I would glide through the streets of Harlem, toward the train station, and emerge in Lincoln Center. It was unheard of for a girl like me to grace any stage, to be warmed by colorful lights, to dance her way to freedom and self-confidence. I loved those shoes. I felt like I put on cement blocks when I had to take my ballet shoes off. These were the shoes that were going to take me to places I couldn't imagine.

But it hadn't worked out that way. I slowly became my worst nightmare. I was plagued with self-doubt. My confidence plummeted, and

I let the streets of Harlem be my comfort. At last, I heard the dreadful words in my senior year: "You will never see the inside of Julliard!" Holy Mother of Curses! Had someone just chain-sawed my legs off? I was a train wreck that had already happened.

I couldn't fix the unfixable. I took my dance degree, shoved it in the back of the closet with the ballet shoes that I wanted to burn, and acted like I'd never loved what saved me from years of misery. On my beat, I imagined walking through the streets with my ballet shoes. Reality would kick in, and the slippers morphed into black boots; the tutu and tights had been replaced by a dark blue uniform and a firearm. I didn't want control, authority and responsibility. I wanted fun, music, and laughter.

"*Hear the beat, of dancing feet...It's the song I love, the melody of...*"

I would feel these words in my own feet, standing on a Times Square corner.

"*Come and meet, those dancing feet...On the avenue I'm taking you to...*"

I'd sing it to myself, looking up at the tip of the George Washington Bridge. The bridge's lights are stars to me; the stars above turn into theater lights. They're all I can see. Through the fog, the white of those lights calms me.

"Non-union dancers, please gather in Studio One."

I am snapped back to the lobby of the audition space. My stomach starts the somersaults, and I have an overwhelming urge to leave. I turn to Candace.

"I can't, I can't!"

"Stop it! You will do fine. I didn't come here with you in the freezing cold for you to quit now."

I give her a hug and follow the waddling line of dancers to Studio One.

All I need is to get through the first audition. Ballet, Jazz, Modern—not a problem. I'm sure of making it to the second level—the singing. That shouldn't be too much of a problem. I am totally coachable, and with the ensemble, I can be drowned out if I sounded like a screeching cat.

I forget about the smell of a studio and ballet shoes while I swing my arms, pose in circus positions, and stare into space.

"*Those dancing feet...*"

I breathe deep, knowing I'll never turn back.

"Ladies, you will be given a short routine to perform as a group; then we will observe you one at a time. If we wish to keep you, we will call your name after everyone has had a chance to perform."

I am totally cool. This is great; we are starting with ballet. I'm sure to make it through.

The woman glances down at her papers and then back up. "Oh, sorry I almost forgot; change into your tap shoessssss…"

To me, this translates to "You are fucked!" I am not a tap dancer. My eyes are burning with sudden sweat, my crotch is completely wet and my heart is beating so fast they could use it as a musical base.

Fuck, fuck, fuck! is the melody going through my head. I told Candace this would be my only downfall, freaking tap. I had dance scholarships! My dancing feet, my ballet shoes, were supposed to get me out of the NYPD and Harlem forever. I thought I'd never have to trade my pinks for the blues again. And now this bitch is telling me to change into my tap shoes!

I slowly pull out my tap shoes, on the verge of tears. I hope that I can at least blend in with the group, and go unnoticed for the routine.

And one, two, three, four, tap, tap, tap, clack slide dig, tap, tap, slide turn, t-tap, t-tap, t-tap…

I instantly turn into a bowling ball, and the other dancers are the pins. Admirably, they are supportive, and I hear them through the noise in my head—"You will get it, don't fret. Just try again." Maybe they know I have no chance, and it costs nothing to throw me a bone.

After grudgingly making it through the group auditions, I scoot into the corner behind the pink human wall and wait for the next order. I am huffing and puffing as though I've just made it out of a shootout alive. I look at my number, 42. That has to mean something. Doesn't it?

"All righty, then. We will call your number. Step to the center of the studio for solos, and nod to the pianist when you are ready."

I want to kill myself. I don't know what is making me stay, except the hope of watching some other dancers make complete fools of themselves. This doesn't happen. Each dancer is better than the one before. By the time they call number 41, I am shaking like a deer that committed a crime and has been caught red-handed by Elmer Fudd. Just like that, Elmer points the shotgun at my terrified eyes and there it is, in slow motion, "N-n-u-u-m-m-b-b-e-e-r-r F-f-o-o-r-r-t-t-y-y t-t-w-w-o-o-o…"

I swallow about a hundred times. The red tape in the center of the studio comes into focus. I wipe my forehead, glance at the judgment table and receive concerned expressions: "We may need an ambulance for this girl."

I nod at the pianist and the ivory hits the air. I flop, twirl, twist, shimmy, give a bit of a hip shake, and pose—*ta-da!*—before the music even ends. The pianist looks over his shoulder and sputters out his last note in amazement. I have turned a simple tap routine into a Barnum and Bailey Circus act.

Dancers are staring at me, open-mouthed, arms across their stomachs. The judgment table is frozen in time. My awkward pose seems to have frozen, too.

In dead silence, a woman at the judgment table stands and claps as hard as she can, blurting out, "YOU ARE SO ADORABLE!"

The room erupts in cheers. In great excitement, I yell, "Can I go to the next level?"

The cheering stops. There are a few uneasy giggles.

"I don't think so dear; but keep training. Come back in a few years."

I walk out of that studio in utter relief.

Ten years later, I see and feel the theatre, the stage, as true to me as oxygen. The universe knows this. My love of dance and music did not come to me by accident. The ballet slippers saved me from early disaster; dreaming big came from the way I feel when I have those slippers on. They are beat up now—battle marks display how hard I've tried.

How I went from dancing to the New York City Police Department is simple: The stage, the attention the drive. Both take immense courage. I never imagined being on stage in the largest city in America. It's a performance, night after night, except no one knows my name after curtain call. My black boots have battle marks, too. Reminds me of how far I have walked. I have grown into a woman on my job; become a wife and a mother—gifts I would have never imagined. My life is meaningful, and the foundation is pretty strong. Sergeant is the rank I hold, with pride. And I still feel like Cinderella. Watching the dancers in the windows of dance schools as I walk my beat is my secret joy.

When I graduated from the Police Academy, I felt like a star. My mother was there. I cried. She was absent for years, but that day, I felt her joy. When I clicked my heels together in the attention position, I looked down and saw my reflected self in the tips of my shoes. They looked just like tap shoes. Frank Sinatra's *New York, New York* started over the speakers in Madison Square Garden, and for a moment I felt my ballet slippers. My name was known after that curtain call; just for that one night.

As I walk down the hallway after my failed audition, my taps echoing on the floor of the audition space, I watch my cousin, wide-eyed, hands together, waiting for the big news. "Well—well? What happened? Are you through?"

Still with the melody in my head. "*On the avenue I'm taking you to...*"

After a deep breath, I say with authority, "Yes. I am."

Toasty Feet Time by Vivien Tartter

Young. Limitless. World-changing. Have it all. Happily ever after. Happily ever after—that was toasty feet time.

Two newly minted doctoral degrees, a young marriage, two careers and lots of possibilities. Yes, we were employed three hours apart, but both jobs were good, mine a hard-to-come by tenure track, and his a general surgery residency. There were two "logical" ways to handle the situation, said our friends: Live somewhere in between and share the commute, or each live near our job and do the weekend marriage thing. I had a different idea of share, the happily ever after idea of marriage and family, to optimize time together.

And so it came to pass that for six years I commuted from New York to Philadelphia, and then 45 min from Philadelphia to Camden and he walked across the street. And while my mostly liberated girlfriends scoffed "this was fair?"—my schedule was regular, his was not; and I never had to return to work at midnight for an emergency. It meant dinner together every possible night, even on-call nights, so long as I and the roast were flexible about the eating hour. Dinner together seemed so important for happily ever after; slaying the dragon Amtrak a trivial detail, for my Prince.

In toasty feet time this sacrifice was appreciated—at least so I recall—and the decision was joint—at least, in my head—but possibly, like happily ever after, that was a convenient fiction. The hardest thing about my commute was predawn awakening for a 10:00 a.m. class, getting to the train station for the 6 a.m. train. Especially hard in the winter, when warm bed-feet were abruptly—no lambs' wool slippers for them!—thrust into cold, tight, high-heeled boots, topped by thin stockings and mini-skirts, then rushed through the frigid pre-dawn air to the subway. And so, for his share of the commute, my Prince drove me three days a week to the train station—no traffic, a 20-minute roundtrip for him, more togetherness, and car heater for my boot-clad feet. Oh yes, toasty feet time. A wonderful time of limitless possibility of home and hearth.

How does one forget that history? How does a couple lose that mutuality? How does it stop being optimal for the us rather than the I? There's a reason fairy tales end right after the wedding.

Mr. Lead and Mr. Blue by Vivien Tartter

Mr. Lead. He must have been one year old or thereabouts, and therefore it was 1987—must have been, since I don't remember worrying about his walking and whether it was too late. Certainly, he was walking, proudly, strutting, all over in his bare feet. Who my first son is now was partly marked then. He walked well way before he let go of the coffee table, physically adept, but cautious and careful. All these years that has not changed. The pride, the strutting, the confidence—that wouldn't be challenged till the double blow in his teenage years of betrayal by Dad and the headmaster (or triple, if you consider the whammy adolescence is on its own when the adult world was simply not to be trusted.) But what lay ahead with no omen in 1987, when he was Adored Child and competent walker, was a very different challenge.

So in 1987 as fall approached, I set out for the big milestone: first pair of shoes. As was the wont of the yuppie class, I went to a child footwear specialist on the Upper East Side, probably not far from where I now buy my overpriced and just as pretentiously fitted running shoes. My son and I were alone. Dad was at work and would have correctly ridiculed the expense of the care of the foot at this shop. Once fitted with both sock and shoe, he was returned to his stroller and strapped in, to sit staring at the new foot enclosures.

We reached a corner and I had an idea! Why not let him walk home in his new shoes? It was only three blocks. So I unstrapped him and stood him up. At the moment I didn't notice the Asian woman, her child or anyone else on the corner.

Adults have walked too long. We have walked barefoot, and in many kinds of footgear. Walking is automatic; we don't think about it.

He stood, feet anchored in lead to the sidewalk. He looked perplexed. He swayed back and forth and in circles—a small bobo punching doll. Larger sway—and fell…flat on his face.

It was then I noticed the Asian woman and her child. Asian mothers are typically very warm and also very overprotective. She looked at me, the abusive mom, in horror. I picked him up, comforted him and returned him to the stroller. I walked home, myself one shoe off and one on, then aware of how differently we move our feet when confined by shoes.

Mr. Blue. A second child is different. As I have said: I will not and did not make the same mistakes; I made different ones…though this is not a story of my mistake, as was the last. A second child, I think, sees the world with less confidence (which may mean, with more reality) and greater longing. Big Brother is always there to show by example superiority and sophistication; maybe some day Little Brother will be as grand. I can't tell if this is true, since I was a first child myself, but at least it fits as behavior model for much of what I see in second son, Mr. Blue.

By the time second son got his first pair of shoes, it was not an orthoyuppie fitting. We knew K-Mart worked fine, and how quickly shoes were outgrown. Nor do I remember whether Mr. Blue was already walking, but I do know he was not yet talking much, and that he was overjoyed at joining the shoe-clad clan. They, the shoes, were white and blue: Hence, Mr. Blue. I still have them, so important a symbol did they seem to be to second son. He could not take his eyes off his feet. Sitting, splay-legged on the floor, he is pictured, touching his Mr. Blue shoes, laughing, proud, looking, looking, looking.

What was so striking? That maybe one day he too would walk, run, jump, pirouette, be a man, like his five-year old brother?

Epilogue. From first shoes those feet have since scored hiking boots, rock-climbing shoes, hockey skates, rollerblades, skis, snowboards, scuba flippers, running shoes, and for older son—steel-tipped boots for construction. Feet, minds, bodies…empowerment.

Photo permission of Vivien Tartter.

These Boots Are Made For Walking by Vivien Tartter
with credit to Nancy Sinatra

I am one of those odd Americans who does a sport for five years before buying the right equipment. (Most Americans, in contrast, begin with all the equipment and then decide they have no taste for the sport.) In the case of hiking, five years is actually an underestimate, since I have hiked all my life, but in the eight years since my husband walked out, the hiking has gotten more serious: longer trips, heavier backpacks, rougher terrain, bad weather as well as good, and camping.

It's odd, the intensification since he left, since it was his sport—he was the one who wanted to rough it; I wanted the nice day hike, hot shower and recoup over a linger-y fine dinner. Over twenty-eight years our personalities crossed, and I guess when the divergence became apparent, maybe the rueful memory of what he was, brought on by his adulthood-approaching sons, and his ever tougher wife—he left, two months after the family hike into and out of the Grand Canyon. It was not the plan to leave the sons, but he never hiked with his family again.

The sons were, as boys are, into all manner of outdoors things—rock-climbing, winter camping, wilderness survival—and in both the spirit of adventure and to grab the last morsels of family life, I joined them as best I could, never sure that this was really me; I didn't buy, but rented, a sleeping bag for our Alaska trip, and refused to get real boots, real waterproof ones, real ones with ankle support, for either of the first two small winter camping expeditions. For those unversed: If your boots get wet in winter camping, they go into the sleeping bag with your body so they don't freeze and can be put on in the morning. Indeed, they can be put on, but they are not warm and dry. If it's not too cold, it's not too bad because hiking is heat generating, but if your feet are cold and wet it is somewhere between unpleasant and dangerous. Thus, the first night my younger son toasted my boots instead of marshmallows by the fire, and, after the second such trip, he insisted I get smart and realize who I am—that in fact *I* do this—and get real boots. In a role reversal that is ever more common these days, he took me to get fitted, and oversaw the purchase of these boots.

Having married at 20, I am single really for the first time in my life, not part of a couple. A few years since the divorce, I stand on my own two feet. Up mountain, down dale, over the river and through the woods, in my hiking boots.

Black Satin Spike Heels by Kathleen Kesson

I was a few months shy of eighteen when I opened in a show at The Golden Hotel and Casino. Too young to come in the front door, I was instructed to slip in the side alley stage door just off Virginia Street and definitely NOT walk by the bar, a prohibition that no one really ever enforced. In fact, I hadn't been there but a week or so when the pit boss started giving me free drink tokens, an incentive to sit out at the bar between shows, presumably to hasten the inebriation of the high stakes gamblers and thus aid the pit bosses in parting them from their money.

I had auditioned for the *Lido de Paris* in Hollywood, in a big old studio on Las Palmas Boulevard where I was taking some acting and dance classes. Weary of the meager living I made doing "serious dance" (Los Angeles Opera Company, festivals, and university performances) I thought I would do something that offered relative financial stability, a three-month run of a big show. Of course, I would have to move to Reno, Nevada for those three months, but the upside was that I could save enough money on my sumptuous $150 a week salary to fund another year of dance and acting classes back in Hollywood.

The revue opened with a Parisian extravaganza performed by the usual late Burlesque cast of characters: the male singer, the female singer, the lead dancer, the lead *nude* dancer, a gaggle of statuesque showgirls in 19th century French promenade gowns, which instead of a conventional bodice, featured their shapely naked breasts set off in elaborate rhinestone frames, and the much shorter, flat-chested, fully-clothed and muscular group of dancers, about ten of us girls, plus Owen and Vince. Owen and Vince were a couple of male dancers thrown in to do the heavy lifting (and tossing about, as it turned out, in the classic French "Apache dance," in which guys demonstrate their affection for their girl friends by picking them up, kicking and screaming, and flinging them to the ground).

I'd been fitted for costumes in Hollywood during rehearsals for the show. The dancer's get-up for the opening number was a traditional can-can costume: A heavily corseted, buttercup yellow cotton dress with black stripes, layers of yellow tulle ruffles underneath, a couple of petticoats, a pert little feather and net hat, the traditional black garter belt and fishnet stockings, and…3½" black satin spike heels.

Yes, spike heels, with a bit of thick elastic around the arch to keep them from flying off during one of those traditional high kicks. Now, in addition to lots of these very high kicks, a can-can dance includes some combination of the following: hopping in a circle on one leg while holding the other leg vertically by the ankle and bringing one's knee close to one's ear, rotational movements of the lower leg with the knee raised and the skirts held high, bending over and showing one's bottom to the audience while tossing one's skirts over one's head, turning cartwheels and flips, and the *grand écart*, a jumping split in the air in which…now picture this…legs at 180 degrees…one holds the split position while crashing down onto the floor. Ouch.

We had rehearsed in the usual attire—leotards, leg warmers, and comfortable ballet or jazz shoes, depending on what number we were working on. I don't recall being particularly daunted by the prospect of performing in spike heels, and, in fact, managed to successfully perform the various acrobatics demanded for the duration of the three months without turning an ankle or damaging forever my potential reproductive capacities. To this day, whenever I hear strains of Offenbach's *Can-Can*, I am transported to that staged scene of Parisian excitement, the swirling skirts, the showgirls in their slightly altered Victorian gowns, the violent Apache dancers. Who is that girl up there, I wonder? I simply cannot fathom this body, this old familiar friend of mine, with its bunions and sore tendons, and shrinking fatty pads and fallen arches and sensible shoes, ever…EVER…actually doing a *grand écart* in ANY sort of footwear, especially not in black satin spike heels. And I'm quite sure that neither my university students nor my colleagues and friends would be able to reconcile these images in their own minds. But there it is. A true shoe story.

Stepping Out in Style—A "Coming Out" Story
by Juliet P. Howard

The moment my eyes looked across the room, I felt the connection instantaneously and knew the attraction was mutual. It was like all the stories I'd heard all those years about hopeless romantics; sometimes you find love when you're not even looking for her. Anyhow, I was flat broke that afternoon and tried not to dwell on my crush. I figured we were just strangers passing in the night, or in our case, in the early afternoon in Greenwich Village. I assumed nothing more would come of our encounter. She was just another crush to add to my freshman list of "firsts" that first year at Barnard. I returned uptown to the campus, to my friends, to my course work, to the busy-ness of an eighteen year old finding her way in a big city. Whenever I had a free moment that semester, my thoughts would inevitably return to her. She was so slender and sexy. There was something masculine, yet ridiculously feminine about her. I loved that she was so androgynous. I couldn't place my finger on it, but every time I thought about my Greenwich Village crush, I had heart palpitations. I became convinced we were meant to be together. I took a part-time job that year, babysitting for the children of a Barnard alum on West End Avenue, just so I could save up enough money to return to the Village one day. I had convinced myself that the next time I went to Greenwich Village, I'd have the nerve to face my crush head on, and that next time I wouldn't be broke.

I remember walking down West 8th Street in search of her. I was nervous and imagined a million reasons this could turn out all wrong: maybe she was gone or maybe I forgot which of those zillion stores on 8th Street that I'd first met her in, or maybe we just didn't fit. As I walked down that street, the heart palpitations returned. But then, there we were, facing each other once again. She was still sitting atop a shelf, glistening in her perfection.

The sales guy jarred me, when he asked, rather impatiently: "Do you wanna try these on? What size you need?"

I could hardly contain my excitement and said "size 7 AA in black please" in a barely audible tone. The sign in front of the store boasted that they sold specialty sizes ranging from triple A to extra wide widths, so my heart was in knots as he went to the back room to search for my size. When he walked out towards me with a white shoe box in his hands,

I was incredibly nervous. He held them out to me, the box top in one hand and the shoes staring up at me, begging for me to try them, in the other hand. Nothing can ever replace that first time I tried on my first pair of black patent leather women's 7AA men's style oxford wing tips. Intuitively, I knew we were meant to be together, and I remember how sweet they felt that first time I tried them. It felt like the first time I had kissed Trina in the women's locker room at Barnard, months earlier. I was tingly all over, in the best possible, *I may explode when this kiss ends*, kind of way. I was excited, nervous and in love. My women's oxford wing tips were slender sexy the moment I slipped my feet in them. It was love at first fitting. The black patent leather glistened and my slender foot felt secure, wrapped in the cocoon of the wing tips. Just the act of lacing up the shoes left me feeling empowered. My footsteps were solid and confident once we were in sync together. So this is what love feels like, I remembered thinking to myself as I floated outside into the busy city streets. "Wings," as I named my sweet new crush, and I, were on our way to conquer the world.

I knew the world would love her as much as I did. It was clear to me everyone would see the beauty, power, elegance and quiet confidence that I saw each time I glanced at Wings. I was so excited to leave the shoe store and show Wings to Mama first, and then later to Trina. I was headed uptown to our apartment in Harlem. Little did I know I was in for a rude awakening back uptown. I remember Mama's voice, loud and angry the first time she noticed Wings.

I was about to step foot out of the apartment, when she screeched: "I know you don't think you are wearing those damn ugly men's shoes outside, do you?" in an angry, arrogant tone, that suggested she was certain she had nipped that nasty little situation in the bud.

"Yes Mama, I have them on because I'm about to go out. I'm meeting Trina and heading back towards campus," I responded, trying to keep my voice level and calm. But underneath, I was pissed off.

It was clear from her expression and tone that Mama hated my shoes. Couldn't she see that these were the absolute most perfect shoes ever? The intercom rang. I buzzed Trina in and ran towards the apartment door, rushing to get there before Mama did. I was trying to get to the door before she said something equally offensive and stupid to Trina. But Mama beat me to the door and pounced on Trina as soon as she rang the doorbell.

"Can you believe these ugly-ass shoes this girl has bought?" she goaded Trina, in search of a confidante. It was Trina's first time seeing Wings and I could tell from the moment she looked down at my feet that she loved them, too.

"Damn, those are beautiful!" she blurted, but realized almost immediately her faux pas. She realized the minute that last syllable slipped off her tongue, that this would mean war with Mama. I saw her bite her lip, struggling with what to say next. She didn't want to offend either of us at that moment. She used her favorite line, one that she had used countless times before on campus when folks had huge disagreements.

"Well, let's just agree to disagree and call it a night." Trina offered her conciliatory advice, along with her charming smile, which begged for a momentary truce.

Mama wasn't letting it go that easily. "Why don't you girls come in for some juice before you head back to campus?" she asked, her tone lighter, calmer. We fell for it and then all sat down in the cramped living room. Mama sat next to me on the sofa, held my hands in hers and literally pleaded with me.

"Why can't you wear more feminine shoes, baby? You would look so much more beautiful and sexy if you wore real ladies' shoes. Please baby, do that for Mama."

I remember looking down at Wings, touching the glistening patent leather, tracing the five eyelets and the black lace that was threaded through each loop and struggling for just the right words.

"Mama, these are ladies' shoes. I mean, no men's shoe comes in 7AA, I'm pretty sure." I smiled, hoping to break the ice of this chilled conversation. "They're just made to resemble men's style Mama, but they're meant for ladies," I offered.

"No, suga, those are men's shoes. Back in the day we called them "bulldagger" shoes. My pretty little girl, ain't no bulldagger is you baby?" she asked, meeting my eyes directly and waiting for an answer.

I could see outside the corner of my eye, Trina squirming uncomfortably in her chair, not at all prepared for such a heavy conversation. I was still reeling over the word "bulldagger" and trying to think how my beautiful, perfect shoes had landed me in the middle of this uncomfortable conversation.

Before I could answer, Mama seemed to have pulled a list from out of nowhere that tumbled from her lips.

"Babygirl, there are a million other shoes for you to wear. You can wear platforms, slingbacks, stilettos, high heeled sandals, even low-heeled espadrilles would soften you up baby, anything but those ugly men's shoes. Your feet are so pretty and petite. Girl, don't you know women would kill to have those slender little feet of yours and show them off? Have you lost your damn mind? What the hell is wrong with you? Did that dyke Trina make you buy those damn men's shoes?!" she snapped, her tone increasingly agitated as she blurted out her thoughts and her fears.

There, she'd said it! She'd offended my lover and me simultaneously.

"Stop it Mama! Stop saying such awful things!" I screamed at her.

"Did Trina make you buy those disgusting shoes? I see how she dresses. Like a little punk-ass tomboy. Did she make you like this?" she grilled me, as she began to shake my shoulders. "Did she turn you into this freak?!" Mama screamed. She was crying and I was crying too.

"We aren't freaks Mama. We love each other. And we're not bulldaggers. We're lesbians," I screamed back at her.

Wow! I couldn't believe I'd said that, I'd finally named who I was to my mama. I was tapping my Wings nervously against the rug, waiting to explode, but I didn't.

Mama tried one final time to make her point: "Those damn men's shoes don't belong on no woman's feet. It's not right! Two women can't love each other!" she screamed, her voice cracking from the screaming and the sobbing.

The "bulldagger" shoes and two women loving each other; somehow we had all become one uncomfortable reality for Mama.

It was then that I realized Mama hated my shoes for the reasons that I loved them. They refused to be categorized. They were a perfect fit on my slender size 7AA feet and though they were indeed women's shoes, they were deliciously boyish and simultaneously sexy. I loved them because they reminded me of why I'd fallen in love with Trina. She didn't fit into a box of what a woman should look or sound like. She was her own person. And those shoes were my first attempt to make a visible stance that I was my own person. I felt really good about the person that I'd become and Wings allowed me to express myself. But unfortunately, all Mama could see was male/masculine/foreign/ unfamiliar/uncomfortable/ ugly/unnatural/other. Mama had figured out that it was women that I loved, and Wings was the final straw. Those wingtips sealed the deal that her baby girl was a lesbian. Yet all Mama wanted was her baby girl back in a rose pink lace taffeta dress, with matching bows wrapped around long ringlets of curls and carnation pink platform shoes to match. She wanted the picture of me trapped in our family photo album, to come back to life. I left that little girl in the Harlem apartment, stored away in the photo book, grabbed Trina's hand and motioned for us to leave. We had all run out of words. Mama sat quietly on the sofa and I reached down and hugged her. I walked confidently, hand in hand with Trina, out the door with both my first loves guiding the way.

Converse-ation Pieces by Stephanie Darrow

It began at age ten, and they were hot pink, high topped. My slender legs dangled off the edge of the tub as I admired them, still on. I wanted to wash them as I washed my own hair now, but my mother said it would ruin them. So, they just waited up in the air, until I was finished.

Throughout secondary school, I adjusted my color tastes regularly and created a healthy balance between low and high tops. As emotional creativity developed, I realized how I could express myself by producing a color on the foot. Luckily for me they were always cheap and available. They were deep purple, bright red, sky blue and all black for almost a year. Eventually they were even rainbow colored, helping me to officially out myself to everyone in my life.

They accompanied neon skinny jeans and worn Alanis Morissette t-shirts; they accompanied black dress pants and collared shirts, even to my cousin's wedding (against my mother's will). They followed me to college and even transitioned to New York City for grad school, although by this time I had toned them down to mostly just black or white.

My shoes. My kicks. I looked down at them on the subway, and felt comforted by their street smudges. I remembered where each marking had come from. The white ones have two small, faint red dots on the side, from a Cosmopolitan spilled on me at a nightclub on Stanton and Rivington. The black ones had an odd yellowish tint on the front, from a Coney Island mustard-topped hot dog. It just gave them character, as quirks do for people.

It seemed to be a perfect love affair, filled with mutual respect, admiration and true love. A relationship that I always thought would last; but, as I blossomed into adulthood (against my own will) I realized that certain aspects of myself were changing. Tastes in foods were expanding. Love for writing even shifted genres. Then, on my twenty-sixth birthday, a sordid realization occurred. Now, my clothing was not only a representation of me, but it was a representation of what I offered. Wow. Okay. Graduate school brought with it interviews, internships, presentations, all that grown up stuff! And there it was. Like Sylvia said: "You do not do, you do not do anymore, black shoe."

She was right. After all these years, I no longer stepped with the same loftiness in arch-less, thin material CT's. I did not see myself in their stark white laces or black threading anymore. I was no longer warm in their vinyl coating and rubber soles. This came as a big surprise to me and I struggled with it at first. I even began to sample what other shoes had to offer. Black leather boots looked great with jeans tucked in them. Sandals were making a big comeback that year. And little slip-on shoes were all the rage. I really felt bad each time I bought a new pair.

As the months went by, I stopped feeling guilty for letting them go. I saw them there, in my closet, every morning when I put on something else. After a while, my guilt for desertion was subsided when I realized my fondness for the shoes would continue, even if their presence did not. So I think back on all of them, each pair that I wore and all the different expressions I made. The British flag ones, when I fell in love with the Spice Girls. The red sequins, when I moved away from home and would say, "Toto, I have a feeling we're not in Florida anymore." And the little hot-pink high tops that I wouldn't take off, not even for a bath. I grew attached to them, and needed them for a million different reasons. Now, although I no longer need them as I had for all those years, I still keep them with all my other shoes, and occasionally bring them out when I'm feeling sentimental. Thanks, Chuck.

My Life in Shoes by Elayne Clift

1946

I stand with my feet in the magic machine that turns my toes a glowing radiation green. The bones look like witches fingers when I wiggle them. I think it is hilarious (I'm only three, after all.) Sometimes I sneak into the shoe store on Broad Street, where my father is the town haberdasher, just to slip my bare feet in the x-ray slots, totally unaware that years from now I could have problems with thyroid cancer. For now, it is the only compensation I have for the dreadful high top, lace up, brown gun boot shoes I am forced to wear because I have that dreaded condition known as "fallen arches."

The only other compensation is that in the summer my mother allows me to buy sandals for our vacation at the beach. Choosing the primary color strapped shoes is sheer happiness. The red, blue, yellow and green straps that weave across my feet, over my toes, and around my ankles fills me with joy, and a love of color such as I cannot otherwise imagine. To this day I thrill to a profusion of such colors.

1950

Finally, I rebel against my military-style footwear. "I'm not going to school in those things!" I wail. My mother relents. I can have saddle shoes with arches inserted, she says. So back we go to the shoe store, where once again I subject my feet to the green machine and am fitted with a spanking new pair of black and white saddle shoes. I'm over the moon at these grownup girl shoes! Loathe to scuff them, I walk carefully, washing away anything that mars their beauty. Eventually I yield to white shoe polish, but once the shoes are "broken in" and molded to my feet, revealing creases across the top, I lose my enthusiasm for them.

That is when, miracle of miracles, my mother says I can have black patent leather Mary Jane's for dress up. Now, nothing in the whole wide world can compete with those delicious shoes. They have a heel higher than anything I've worn before, and a black grosgrain ribbon at the toes. I feel like Cinderella at the ball!

And I'm up to three pairs of shoes in my closet: saddles, sandals, and shiny patents. What girl could possibly ask for more?

1958

The junior high prom is upon us. With support from my older sister who's been dating regularly for years, I screw up my courage and call my not-so-secret heartthrob. He accepts my invitation to escort me to the ball. I hardly feel like Cinderella now. I'm convinced that I'm the ugly one masquerading as my beautiful step-sister.

My sister hauls me off to buy a dress and shoes for the big event. The dress we choose is a red dotted-Swiss affair, with a large white eyelet cummerbund at the waist and mounds of fullness to the skirt. Sleeveless and cut in a V at the bodice, it is something to behold.

But it's the white shoes we buy to go with the red and white dress that convince me I can pull this event off with all the sophistication of my older, more experienced sister. The shoes are pumps with rounded toes, white bows at the point where they meet my feet, and my first real pair of heels. I've had a pair of blue pumps prior to this extravagance which I wore to a funeral, but they were starters with small, tapered heels; something akin to starter bras for budding debutantes.

On the night of the dance, I descend the stairs—we always descended the stairs then to meet our dates—my shiny white heels gracefully taking the lead. My red and white wrist corsage is perfect, and off we go, to dance the night away. My friends at the prom barely comment on my dress, but they are totally impressed by my white heels.

1964

In college, Capezios are the thing. They accessorize our matching wool skirts and sweaters with their daintiness, and we try to have at least two pairs in different colors. When winter comes, and we are forced into boots to trudge to school in the bitter Boston cold, we put the Capezio lovelies into their boxes, to be stored until spring. A few clever girls, clearly ahead of their time, carry their Capezios in their handbags, removing their boots as soon as they are inside a building where they can once again trip the light fantastic. But most of us wait for spring to come, then, with great excitement, ritually break out the Capezio boxes. It is a passage in its own right.

1975

I am working for a feminist organization, where blue jeans and T-shirts are the norm. But I'm not quite there. We are living in Washington,

D.C. and my husband is a diplomat. We are often called upon to attend evening events, at which I am expected to look and behave as "wife of." Besides, I've been working for several years, always in settings where "dress for success" is the code. So I continue to wear handsome suits with plain pumps, or at the very least, a skirt, a blouse and some modest jewelry. Eventually, my colleagues get used to it and stop intimating that I'm not really a feminist. I concede only insofar as to bring back my Capezio look. They're feminine and flat. There is, at least, that.

Certain occasions connected to my husband's work call for more: dressy clothes and high-heeled pumps, at the very least. At this point, I buy my first and only pair of the shoes known by my friend Ellen as "Fuck Me Shoes." They are black patent leather, stiletto-heeled, strapped affairs, and I can barely walk in them. I wear them once, and years later, retrieving them from the back of my closet, dump them ceremonially in the trash.

By this time, I am the mother of two young children. My work shoes are flatter, and on the weekends I wear sneakers. My colleagues think there may be hope for me yet.

1998

My husband has retired; I can tele-commute, now that my career involves teaching and writing, and, desperate to escape the political landscape of Washington, we move to rural Vermont. The first thing we do is buy snowshoes, cross-country skis, and boots that are so heavy-duty they are difficult to lift. The first time my niece sees my husband in his boots, she howls with laughter. "I never thought I'd see my uncle be a shit-kicker!"

I also buy moccasins, and slip-on slippers. In Vermont, everyone checks their shoes at the door and slides into slippers. It is a wonderfully cozy ritual, and we do it year-round. In 2005, when I live in Thailand to teach for a year, the requirement to remove shoes at the door is entirely normal to me.

I also buy my first pair of Naots, the Israeli brand of healthy shoes that competes with Birkenstocks and other manufacturers of that ilk. I'm not used to buying such expensive shoes, but never have I felt so comfortable. After a few years, I'm on my fourth pair, and my arches are no longer falling! Now, that's shoes!

Naots, oh so comfy.

Photo permission of Elayne Clift

2012

I haven't worn a pair of heels in over fourteen years. I only own one pair now, black patent leather pumps, just in case there is a wedding or funeral and my Capezio flats would seem slightly inappropriate (although I almost exclusively wear trousers now). I'm still wearing Naots, sneakers and slippers. My feet are happier than they've ever been.

It's been quite a shoe journey since those gun boot days, and, while I may not have walked in another man's shoes, I've traveled far and well in my own. Now that I think about it, I realize that my footwear has marked the milestones of my life. Who'd have thought that possible in the days of green toes, colorful sandals, and shiny black patent leather Mary Janes?

Time Steps by Estha Weiner

She always told me: you can tell a well-dressed woman by her shoe wardrobe. Words to live by, and though she feared living, she did live up to those words. Her shoes were always from Saks Fifth Avenue, although Maine was her home. They were purchased on the few vacations she took to New York with my father, or ordered by mail through one woman, Mary Brett Hale, long before there were personal shoppers in fancy department stores. Mary Brett Hale knew her size, and her taste, and that the shoes had to be made with Fenton lasts, whatever those were. They were in excellent taste, fine leather with stacked heels, usually in shades of taupe, black, and red, and always spectator pumps for spring: navy and white, black and white. Then there were the black suede high heels, a few bejeweled, the pink and black boudoir slippers, and a wonderful surprise: black and red dancing shoes that tied seductively around with ankles with a velvet ribbon. Though her weight rose and fell throughout the years, her upper thighs keeping her from bathing suits, her calves remained shapely and attractive, like mine, people say. From the tips of her toes to the tops of her knees, at least, she was always perfect.

This was shown off to best advantage when she danced, which she did with great flair and grace, in her kitchen, always a shocking break, like her flashes of humor, from her usual depressive rhythms.

The dancing classes she had taken in her youth served her well, the doctors said, after her first operation. There was still residual muscle strength from the rigors of training past. But they had to amputate anyway, from the knee down. Unattended diabetes had taken its toll. Next came the loss of three toes on her other foot, and gradual loss of vision.

When still further medical complications made it impossible for her to live, even with help, at home, we found her an extended care facility, another name for nursing home. But we always kept the hope alive that she would return to her own home, when she was better.

Costs for her care kept mounting, and costs for maintaining her own home, which now lay fallow, except for our occasional visits, remained a constant. The care facility sustained her health, but couldn't force her to practice walking with the prosthesis, or to push herself in any way. She did not get better.

We put her home on the market, but after months without an offer, rented it to a young family, who wanted it unfurnished. We packed her life in boxes. Her shoes filled two cartons, like living dead bodies, black, taupe, red, and spectator pumps for spring. The only pair that fit me was the black and red dancing shoes, which now sit in my shoe rack, standouts, in a far less illustrious collection.

Black Sparkle, Black Stardust by Alyssa Yankwitt

They had a two-inch heel and a strappy bridge of black glitter over the open toes. My first pair of Salsa shoes. I felt fabulous wearing them, fierce. Dressed in a liquid silk gown, black as ink; my mouth, a red Cuban Hibiscus. My hips spun like Lucille Clifton's, while a tall, dark Latino whirled me across a dance floor. That was the woman I was while wearing the shoes, but that's not who I really am.

My Salsa class was Sunday nights and it was my one hour a week where I wasn't a teacher, or a bartender, or a girlfriend. In fact, I wasn't anything, except a girl learning to dance. I always loved to dance, had taken tap, jazz, and ballet as a girl. My childhood dream was to be a Rockette; however, at 4'10, that was never going to happen. My other love in life is Spanish culture and music. While I figured out the rhythm of Salsa from the music, I finally wanted to learn the rules. Intrigued by a dance where the man leads, the other appeal was partnering. Salsa revolves around the woman, but she succumbs to the man's whims. In my daily life, I am usually the one in control. So staunchly independent, I wasn't sure that I could give up that control and let someone else, a man no less, lead.

So, on Sunday night, I put on my Salsa heels, and went to class. There were no gowns of black silk, red lips, or handsome Latinos to whirl me around. But there were others, like me, who didn't want to discuss their careers, who wanted to leave their lovers and spouses at home—who just wanted to dance. And we did. I found the rhythm instantly and my feet loved "Black Sparkle and Black Stardust," constantly craving the movement. My body, legs, hips, thighs, found comfort in patterns of back two-three, front two-three, back two-three, front two-three. My toes, always perfectly pedicured, peeked out from the black glitter as I spun across the floor. We never had the same partner, constantly changing from song to song. While my fantasy partner was tall, dark, and Spanish, my favorite partner in class was tall, gangly, and Serbian. His name was Goran and he resembled Ichabod Crane. He was the last person I thought would ever be able to lead me. But he did.

Even in my heels, I barely reached Goran's shoulders; our bodies moved with the fluidity of a river, and yet a calculated synchronicity. Very gently, Goran partnered me, guiding me through careful signals, pulls and pushes, firm but not too firm, secure, but never tight. And I responded—changing my feet from front and back to left to right, arm loop or sombrero, when needed. Occasionally, my eyes wandered from Goran's lanky frame down to the floor, where a glint of Salsa shoe sparkle would catch my eye. It was this flick and spark of heel that instantly transformed me into the impassioned salsera I imagined myself as.

One evening, so caught up in the moment, the music, the *salsera*, I lost count of my steps, couldn't retrace the beat to the tapping of my heels. During a cross-over step I lost my balance; my left foot, instead of crossing over my right, knocked it completely out of position. The twinkle of glitter from the shoes hit my eye just as my toe spun out. Then I was on the ground. I could hear some stifled laughter and a few *are you OK's?* as I sat, stunned, on the wooden floor, trying to figure out what happened. It wasn't so much embarrassment from falling that had unnerved me; it was that I had let my partner down. But just as that thought appeared in my head, Goran appeared, his awkward frame leaning over me, arm extended toward mine. He gently took my hand, helping me to my feet. My eyes traveled upward, from my shimmering Salsa shoes to Goran, who smiled kindly at me. Without a word, he placed his right hand on my back, placed his left hand over my right, began dancing with me once again. We fell back into the movement as though we had never stopped.

"Thanks," I said softly, beneath the music.

Photo permission of Alyssa Yankwitt

"We're a team," he said in his thick accent, slowly turning me left as my shoes tapped in time to the music, in time to my heart. I was learning how to be a partner.

Walk More, Imagine More.
Cuanto Mās Caminas, Mās Imaginas. by Carla Porch

Ten days after the spring equinox, I was in my patio garden assessing what plants had survived the long, frigid winter when I looked up and saw evidence of life returning: verdant buds had sprouted on the bare, ashen branches of the neighbor's birch. I felt relieved it had survived, since it is not planted in the ground, which would insulate its roots from freezing temperatures, but in a wooden planter filled with potting soil that sits on the cold cement patio floor. As soon as all the birch's leaves had dropped in late fall, a very cold winter arrived, weeks ahead of schedule, and the tree went into the deadliest-looking stage of dormancy I had ever seen it in; I thought for sure it had died. When these buds transform into leaves, the birch will become a grand presence in my garden without any tending from me. It is planted just on the other side of the garden wall I share with its owner.

The exceptionally balmy tail end of March allowed me to wear flip-flops when I came out, rather than my gardening clogs. Despite an encroaching dampness, warmth from both the radiant heat emanating from the cement floor and from the shift in seasons lingered in the air. Spring had arrived; winter was gone for sure. And this would have been one of the times of year when my mother would offer to buy me footwear—sandals for spring, shoes or boots if it was fall, or workout sneakers whenever I needed them. She had never placed a limit on how much she was willing to pay, or perhaps, the shoes she bought me never cost beyond what she was willing to spend. I never questioned her as to why she hadn't abandoned our ritual once I had become an adult and had long since been able to afford buying my own shoes. She didn't have to be with me when I found the right footwear, either. If I told her over the phone I'd found something I liked, she'd pay me back for the shoes next time I saw her. But when we went shopping together and I spotted the right shoes on display, she would encourage me to try them on, and, if they fit and suited my feet, she'd offer to buy them.

Overhead, gray clouds began to envelope the enduring, cerulean sky of the last few days, and the temperature dropped. I went inside and went directly to my closet. Bending down to the shoe shelf below the row of hanging clothes, where the sandals from previous summer seasons awaited at far end of the shelf, I asked, "Which ones of you will I wear again, and which ones of you will go to Salvation Army and be replaced?"

⚚

I sat in my blue writing chair, feet propped up on the matching ottoman, my writing journal opened in my lap, pen nib pressed next to the word "replaced." Emptiness had seized me where the words for stories come from: the pen had remained at a standstill for the last few days.

At first, I thought the culprit was the burgeoning, imbalanced, confused hormones of pre-menstrual syndrome. After my hormones retracted, in unison, I suppose, my period arrived, cramp-free, but not the words to follow "replaced."

I didn't even try sitting in my blue writing chair the next morning. Instead, I went out to my patio garden and pulled dead plants from pots, pruned what was coming back, calculated how many to replace, and swept and hosed the floor. I spent the rest of the afternoon going over my garden diary entries of what plants grew well and which did not thrive here, then created a list of flowers and herbs to buy at the nursery. The next morning I drove there and returned with all the plants on the list. By dusk the garden was complete; its revitalization had replaced two days of writing. I felt a familiar sense of accomplishment; planting provided me the same satisfaction as completing a story. All the plants would need from now on would be watering, if it didn't rain, and occasional weeding and deadheading until late fall, when the plants in the garden would return to dormancy, or death.

Rather than attempting to write the next day, I removed dead leaves from the indoor plants, and transferred those that had grown too large for their existing pots into larger ones. I had put on music beforehand— instrumental only. Though I wasn't writing, I would adhere to my writing rule: no music with vocals, for I can't write when I hear another voice. I selected *The Sea*, a Scandinavian quasi-classical ensemble featuring electric rock guitar. As the opening piano chords struck on an early track, evoking waves hitting rocks along a shore, the entering drum rhythms incited my breath to follow in same the beat. Cello strums enhanced reverberation; and when the electric guitar riffs followed, I went into a reverie. I felt myself floating between two fjords, causing me to drop the clump of dead leaves in my palm and go over to CD jewel case and pull out the liner notes, which I'd never before thought to read. At the top of the first page was an epigraph, taken from Kafka's *The Silence of the Sirens*;

Now the sirens have a still more fatal weapon than
their song, namely their silence. And though admittedly
such a thing has never happened, still it is conceivable
that someone might possible have escaped from
their singing, but from their silence certainly never.

❧❧

I made a concoction of flower essences and water in a final attempt to dissolve this block within my psyche, which I had diagnosed as a "Pattern of Imbalance" from the labels on the bottled flower essence. Perhaps the silence to the right side of "replaced" could be transformed to proliferation with these elixirs: Iris, it was claimed, *"elevates the lack of inspiration or creativity and the feeling of being weighed down by the ordinariness of the world;"* Wild Oak addresses *"confusion and indecision about life's direction;"* and two drops of the Lady Slipper *"transforms the estrangement from inner authority and the inability to integrate higher spiritual purpose with real life and work."* All three conditions were mine. While I released two drops each of Iris, Wild Oat, and Lady Slipper into the glass of water, I asked, "Can I get beyond the closet, and maybe into a shoe store?" I sat in the blue chair to sip the concoction. A numbing sensation covered my face and eyelids as the residual memory from a recent dream appeared in my mind's eye.

❧❧

I returned to the shoe store where I bought last fall's gift from my mother. The company's motto is: *Walk more. Imagine more.* How simply put, and maybe, a necessity. Maybe walking more would dissolve this threshold of wordlessness that I'm reluctant to cross. I've read once that the mind can imagine up to 3.5 miles per hour while the body walks.

I scanned the rows of shoes and sandals displayed for the spring season and didn't like what I saw. None were appropriate for my feet, except for maybe the last pair next to where the men's selection began; they were flats, styled after a ballet slipper. The sides had open slits and so did the top, which configured into a lotus blossom revealing the tops of the toes. These were not quite shoes, nor a sandal. I asked the clerk, who had been at my side as soon as I entered the store, "May I see these in black, size ten?" He returned with a pair in blue. "Try these on. If you like how they fit, I can order a pair in black." They held my toes and the back of my heel just right. The innersole molded to the bottom of my foot, adding a layer of cushioning that felt snug. I walked around the store in comfort and ease, but would I imagine more? No words had been added to the story; "replaced" remained the last.

The following week, the shoe store called to let me know the size ten black slippers had arrived. The male voice on the other end called them *Casi Nada*, adding, "We will hold them for twenty-four hours." I hadn't known the name of the shoe style, but, of course, they would have a Spanish name: the company that made them and owned the shop was headquartered in Spain. As I placed the receiver into the phone cradle, I translated: "Almost Nothing." The week-old numbness left my face.

I returned to the shoe store the next afternoon. An unfamiliar sales clerk approached me at the entrance and asked if I needed help. Looking at him, I realized I was old enough to be his mother. I shifted from knowing why I had come here to feeling confused and unstable on my feet; for a second, I didn't know where I was. I turned my head, caught my image in a long vertical mirror on the far wall, and saw my mother's gaze: a gaze that could range from lively, transparent, and full, to deadening, opaque, and small. Her final gaze, before she died, the irises and pupils had become one, a merger of black opacity—a gaze that no longer gave, nor could receive. Now, this gaze was coming from me. Was that how the clerk saw me? I responded, "Yes, you are holding a pair of shoes for me."

The clerk returned from the storage room with a brown shoebox. He lifted the lid and turned the box horizontally to show me the contents. I noticed the thin tissue shrouding the shoes tightly together had never been unfolded, then refolded. They had never been taken out of the box since they'd left the factory in Spain. No one else's feet had been in them before. I felt honored.

As I opened my hands to receive the box, I looked up at the clerk to thank him, and realized I had seen him before, in a dream; he was a young teenager who had taken up residence in my mother's house after she had died. His turned-up nose was the giveaway, as well as his hairstyle: short wisps, springing around his ears and falling down his neck in scalloped layers. He had made an espresso on my mother's stove, and had offered me a sip from his cup. Here as a shoe clerk, he had grown up. His hazel eyes twinkled at me as he placed the shoebox in my hand.

I sat on a bench along the wall, still holding the box horizontally. A voice spoke within me, "You don't need them and you shouldn't spend the money. They're not sandals and they won't be practical once it gets warm. They'll make your feet hot." Overruling the voice, I unveiled the left shoe first, because it would determine the proper fit; like most people, my left foot is slightly larger than the right. I sat the box, with its shrouded right mate, next to me, removed my left shoe and sock, then slid on the slipper.

෧෴

A blizzard came in mid-April. Heavy, draping snow covered much of my garden; only the buds opening to green leaves of the birch peeked through the dense white. The scene added doubt and confusion about keeping the *Casi Nadas*. I had yet to wear the slippers out of my apartment, since I was considering returning them. I sat in my writing chair, rubbing the terry cloth innersole with my toes, rationalizing the lining would keep my feet cool when it was hot.

෧෴

I had set the alarm for 5:30 a.m., in hopes that if I saw the light of dawn it would fuel me with inspiration. At 7:00 a.m., I could not get beyond the word "slipper."

"Those shoes cost $140?" my mother would have said. "That's a lot, but they do look nice on your feet. They make them look smaller." My mother could never get over that my feet had grown to a size ten; her shoe size was eight and a half, from young adulthood till death.

"Yes, because foot and shoe have become one. The slippers are called 'Almost Nothing,'" would have been my response to her.

"So, what's the point of the story?" I asked myself.

Silence. No word came to my hand on the page. Only *Casi Nada* came to mind. *Do I keep the not-quite-sandals, not-quite-shoes? $140 is too much for slippers.*

I picked up one of the *Casi Nadas* from the shoebox next to my writing chair. One day remained, to decide if I would keep them, or return them and get my money back. I held the front of the slipper in my left hand as the fingers on my right caressed the texture of the sole, rubbing what felt like letters of the alphabet. I flipped the shoe over and saw that the letters had been randomly molded into the rubber sole. Amid the random pattern, I could decipher a sentence, a message:

El hombre es el unico animal que tropieza dos veces con la misma piedra.

Man is the only animal that stumbles twice with the same stone.

Once Upon a Time... by Lynn Dion

Once I wrote a fairy tale.

This is not unusual in itself. People often write them for their own children, or for the children of others. Less often, people write them as assignments, as I did after the initial shock of signing up for a course in children's literature and finding out I was expected to produce the stuff, not just analyze it.

I discovered that a fairy tale is not just any story. It's a projective adventure for the writer as well as the reader, and many things not consciously intended may float up, disguised in dreamlike and seemingly irrelevant forms. When this happens, the whimsical characters and their puzzling narrative may suddenly show themselves as closely true, maybe too closely to lie within normal sightlines.

Guillemot, the princess in my tale, begins as a sheltered little being:

The princess was so carefully cherished that she was never permitted to go beyond the courts of the palace or even to walk upon the bare earth...her thin court slippers were cloth-of-gold, and she trod only on the finest carpets and smoothest marble of the palace.

Well—that's how she starts out. Barely born at eighteen, tenderly shod in golden shoes even though she can hardly walk at all. Never so much as chips a toenail on a stone in the garden, nor ever expresses any desire to put her bare feet to the grass, the sunny rock, the chilling sea strand. When the inevitable comes—a tidal wave like the one that drowned Atlantis—and Guillemot is separated from her royal parents and all their soft and restrictive comforts, her useless golden slippers are torn away by the freezing flood. And when she is cast up on land she follows a narrow and overgrown path, her bare feet bleeding, to a life of deprivation and hard work.

She is rewarded for her first small triumph:

As Guillemot began to sweep the cellar floor, the bristles at the end of the broom gave off a faint glow, and she saw the mice and beetles, and the ancient filth, giving way before it. Turning, she could barely make out the shining eyes of a stubby gray rat. He spoke: "Sweep all the way to the far wall, and you shall find your reward." She swept and swept. When she reached the far wall she was very hungry, and she found a round stone crock with sweet carrots and tender young beets inside it. She also found a pair of leather shoes, fine but sturdy, and they fitted perfectly.

She moves forward, passing through sexual awakening to a clear-eyed engagement with the life of her mind. And in the pattern of the tale, good nourishment and practical gifts are bestowed on her every time. But her first reward, won by overcoming the fear of being on her own and clearing away the outworn, received clutter that fills the deep foundations of her world, is a pair of well-made shoes—made, it seems, for her alone.

Did I have any idea as I wrote it that it was the story of my own youth and liberation? Not exactly. Or rather yes, exactly—with great precision—but not consciously. The first act of the fairy-tale Guillemot, when she escapes the loving, tight leash of her royal keepers, is to ground herself in her new existence with work, like me, and find an unexpected reward in sweet new roots and footwear such as she has never dreamed of wearing before. (Quite a lot of it, really—I remember being particularly shoe-crazy that first year on my own.) And so, once the task of separation is irreversibly underway, the tale recounts something formative—tentative, yes, but real—reflected in a hazy looking-glass that had at first returned no image at all:

Before she went to her tiny chamber, she crept into the secret room and stood before the mirror. It was still clouded with the swirling mist, but suddenly she could see her own pretty legs and feet, with the fine and sturdy shoes upon them.

Some of the shoes I collected in the first few years after leaving home were fad-stylish or funky (we're talking about the early 70s), pure impulse purchases. Sometimes they were failed experiments, fun to look at in a store window, but impractical or even uncomfortable to run around in. But a significant number of them were formative in some important way, symbols of an odd, bottom-up awareness that grew eventually into a fine and sturdy sense of myself, and anchored all the shifting roles I was growing into.

I bought the moccasins within a week of moving away from home and into the dormitory of the nursing school attached to the hospital that provided my first job. The nursing school enrollment had dropped off over the years, so single rooms were available to female employees, and my parents reckoned it was safer than a regular apartment. For my part I was happy it was in another city.

The rear boundary of my college was an easy walk from the hospital, down a tree-shadowed, dead end street, under a fence, over a broad, pathless oak-and maple-wooded plot and across the athletic fields of the school. That first windy fall, the brilliant foliage and the tannic reek of the rotting leaves were intoxicating. I even savored the scramble over roots, acorns and little rocks underfoot, coming through the woods.

The moccasins had something to do with that. I had grown up seeing those flat-soled, pastel-colored slippers with fringes at the ankle that are called moccasins, but these, which I had picked up as an oddity from a hippie shoemaker at a fair, were the real thing. They didn't even have a right or left to the pair, and the bottoms, a thick cowhide that wrapped right around from the laced tops, were not soles to speak of—the whole thing was more like a leather sock with a laced-up top and a semi-formed heel. The maker told me I had to mark them left and right, and they would conform with wear to the unique shape of each foot. How strange, how primitive and eccentric. I was enchanted at once.

And so I trudged to classes and back, deeply contented both coming and going, and with something like bare feet to the earth for the first time, forming the unformed shoes to be my own, getting tougher and balancing better on the knobby, broken terrain every day. It never occurred to me to fear the early dark under the trees as the weeks passed. With heavy socks and a good mink oil rubbing the mocs went well into early winter, and I laid them down only when the first big snow fell.

Nursing was our family tradition, and big, rounded Clinic oxford shoes are a fixture in my earliest memories. I was working at the hospital where my sister trained, and there were lots of people who knew her, so I was accepted and probably sheltered a bit more than the average new aide at the beginning.

I worked all-night shifts, which gave me the room I needed to plan an irregular schedule of daytime classes and evening rehearsals as a music major. On the night shift the staff is small, and the shift is uneventful most of the time. I made rounds with a flashlight, solemnly padding along the dim, rubber-tiled corridors in my crisp new uniforms and big Clinic shoes, feeling nurse-y and looking quite the part. The RNs taught me to take a reliable patient history and vital signs, and then I was allowed to admit patients too, if they happened to come in at that time of night.

One night a patient I had just admitted exploded behind my back as I turned to leave his room. I don't mean he shouted—I mean in five seconds' time he went from paper white and already drifting off to sleep, to a battlefield's worth of blood and misery. An elderly end-stage alcoholic, he had erupted into a projectile upper gastric bleed and was covered in clots and worse, beyond my ability to take in. I truly believe it was the shoes holding me vertical.

He comforted me first, and so I was able to begin positioning and cleaning him. I hadn't even been taught how to change an occupied bed, and I was soon covered in the mess. Afterwards, I scrubbed the snappy new uniform in vain; but the shoes wiped clean. My sister had counseled me how to care for them, including regular polishing and waxing, and the bloody residue had not even stained the ropy saddle-stitching. It took my appalled heart longer to come clean; the uniform never did. But the shoes walked me through the next night, and the next.

A voice major is always in the chorus. What else are we good for? That was how some of the instrumental players thought of us—actors who sang, but not real musicians. Bad readers, and pathetically stupid in harmony and orchestration.

I am here to tell you we worked damned hard, and we were the ones whose instruments were our very bodies. (I can tell you too that I was a fine reader and especially sharp at analysis of form, but that's getting off the point.) When we performed the big works for chorus and orchestra, the women of the chorus truly suffered, crammed onto narrow risers and standing composed and motionless for half an hour or more, in pointy, pretty pumps. Many of us wore flat ballet slippers instead, which looked all right, we thought, from out front and at least didn't make anyone come close to fainting with pain. But sure enough, the director (a man) eventually told us the slippers were ridiculous even under the long black gowns, and demanded that we wear a decent looking dress shoe with some kind of heel to it. The bastard.

My trip to hunt down a shoe both pretty and bearable to get me through the Mozart Requiem was dismal. I was innocent as an egg in those days, but even I knew the salesman in the last possible store was a guy who liked his job, and especially the foot-fondling part. Still, the boxes were piling up around us and he was growing exasperated, and I had to tell him what the problem was. The transformation was astonishing: he rose up on his toes, fingertips together, and exclaimed, "But I know exactly what you need! You should have told me!"

Before I could utter another word, he had taken out some measuring devices and was fitting me for a pair of Capezio tap shoes. The store had a fair clientele of dancers and the stock was large. He swept away the boxes of rejects and cleared my path to a revelation: a shoe that was femmy enough for Ruby Keeler in spangles, but steel-shank supported, roundish and roomy at the toe, and deceptively broad and sturdy at the heel, where it counted the most. We decided on the two-inch heel with the narrow throat strap.

"Now, that's a WORKING shoe for a girl," he declared. "When's the concert? Good, come back tomorrow to pick these up. You won't want the taps, but I'm going to put Cat's Paw soles on so you'll never slip climbing on risers."

I kissed him on the cheek. "I'm sending some friends," I murmured. He smiled and gave me a small sheaf of his cards.

৵৽

Conducting takes presence and command quite apart from the technical skill. Everyone in a performance effort is important, but not everyone is cut out to lead. Some of us are a little more precarious as leaders. When the work is going well, the rank and file will follow and great things may be accomplished; but if we lose confidence, they can feel it, and the show will threaten to disintegrate.

In my third year I discovered I loved conducting more than almost anything, and the fact that I was a sometime leader took no edge off the desire. The way I acquired my first baton is an indicator of how much I wanted it. I am not a sneak by nature, but this came close to despicable. The day the teacher brought the bundle of sticks to class and we all began swinging them like flyswatters, another student handed me his and said, "I might like this one—what do you think?" I knew the moment I picked it up that it was for me. They all looked alike, but the weight and balance were infinitely varied, and this one was perfection. I said, "Too light. You want something with more heft. It'll fly right out of your hand! Try this one." And I handed him the unresponsive splinter of kindling I had been flailing with. He took it, pleased, and said, "Gee, thanks!"

In that same term, I began to wear big wooden clogs for the first time. I had never wanted them; I had merely tried on my deep chestnut-brown pair in a store to humor a friend. But because I was fighting that semester to find my center as a director, the sudden sensation of solid blocks of wood under my feet, and the slight shift in even my visual perspective on having my whole foot rise, not just the heel, and bring me to a different height, caught my attention hard. Laugh if you like: it was a personal, portable podium. I had never had anything so solid and unyielding under my arches as those chunks of birch; I felt them up my entire spine and the posture followed through and emanated from my very eyes.

They worked. They worked like the stone in stone soup; they worked because I already had the goods and I just needed a lucky piece, like some home-run-hitter. They worked because the insistent platform that moved with me as I moved, the touch of strange that became my feet took me out of myself and gave me wholly to the work at hand. They worked because we don't just make metaphors of the concrete; sometimes we take it back the other way from figurative to literal, and I felt the director's privilege as ground, moving under me and abiding in those shoes.

The princess herself has long since taken charge of writing the tale. When she was still young and running over the marble floors of the parental palace, she sometimes exchanged her golden court slippers for red leather oxfords that she wore to the royal school (without touching the ground between the palace and the brick schoolhouse across the street). A higher grade every autumn, bigger feet, harder and better books, and apple-red tie shoes, still unscuffed in the box, with a deep leather glow like the glow of polished buckeye chestnuts. Those red shoes, faithfully replaced each year, were the hope of someday learning enough to be released into the wide world.

Now the fairy tale girl is finishing another of her mad collection of those things the world calls a "degree," and already wondering what her next learning project is going to be; but finishing one cycle of learning and starting another demands red shoes, that much is perfectly clear.

On the table in front of me is a new pair of Danish clogs. The color label on the box reads "Chili Pepper." They are a brilliant scarlet suede with the new lightweight sole; it's hard to find wooden soles on clogs any more, but my feet are decades older and they appreciate the update in comfort. What hasn't changed is the way the clogs raise me above the floor and up onto a personal podium. The illusion is still strong, and there is more than one thing a person can do from that height. I'll teach from it—they'll never know.

March 15 Meets Chiron the Wounded Healer
by Suzanne Weyn

March 15. It's rainy and cold. Midterm astronomy report is due, but I'm staring out the window. I've gotten as far as getting onto the Internet to do some research. It's either stare at the rain or stare at the screen. Not much choice.

I'm aware that it's March 15 because we have just finished reading Shakespeare's *Julius Caesar* in my English class. I didn't love it, except for the part where they stab Julius. That was pretty dramatic. He should have worn some armor or just stayed home, because it's not like he wasn't told. The seer warned him: Beware the Ides of March. And even then he was smug about it. He says to the seer: "See? It's March 15 and nothing's happened. To which the seer replies, more or less—"It's not over 'til it's over."

Having stared at rain-soaked apartment houses for as long as humanly possible, but not ready to end the procrastination, I hit the horoscope link and go to Cancer, my sign. *Today Mars intersects with Chiron the Wounded Healer. You may be ambushed by painful memories from your past.* No kidding. That's what it said. Jumped from behind, just like Julius.

Beware. Be wary.

I Google Chiron and get a load of info. It's a remnant of a comet that got caught in our solar system. It's in an egg-shaped orbit around Saturn and Uranus. I wonder if I could do my report about it.

The story about Chiron, the mythological character for which it's named, is interesting. Chiron was a centaur, one of those half human, half goat, or half whatever, creatures from Greek mythology. He was abandoned by his parents and didn't fit in with the other centaurs because he was a more reflective, sensitive type. He seemed doomed to be flattened by life—steamrolled, mashed—but he fooled everyone. He grew up to be a wise healer, a teacher, and everyone came to him for advice.

So now I have an idea, at least. I'll write this astronomy report on Chiron and get the thing over with. Before too long, I have three pages worth. I like the idea of a planetoid out there that's really from another solar system. Another solar system! The universe is so vast that it shatters my mind when I think about it. My head actually starts to hurt.

My cell phone rings, and it's my mother. We need chopped meat for supper. Can I go get some? And some milk. And can she borrow the money for it from me, until the end of the week? "Sure," I agree with a sigh.

I hang up and get my jacket. It's not really pouring, but it's windy and wet. I don't want to go out. Plus, I'm not crazy about spending my last twenty bucks on meat and milk.

Out on the street, it's colder and wetter than I expected. People walk along with their heads ducked down. And then, all of a sudden, the sky just opens up as if someone is dumping buckets of water down.

I jump back into the doorway of a store to get out of it. It's one of those big, brightly lit stores that sell all sorts of clothing and furniture and this and that. Shaking the rain from my hair, I figure I'll go in and browse around until the rain lightens up.

They have fashions that my mother would like, but nothing I really want. There's a section with these big, goofy hats—I guess because Easter is coming, and some women still wear Easter hats. One section is stuffed with white communion dresses—big, poofy, beaded white gowns for little girls. They're pretty, and before I know it, I'm checking through them and remembering when I was seven and made my first holy communion.

As I remember all this, the lights in the store suddenly seem too bright, and I recall that I have to get that meat and milk. I'm about to leave, when I notice a display of shoes. Gorgeous, shiny patent leather pumps; opened toed with high, high heels. And there is a red pair that I have to have. Fifty percent off! Only $19.99.

I turn them in my hand. That's when something I have totally forgotten comes blasting into my head. It's a picture of another pair of red shoes from long ago.

Back when I was seven, I had wanted a pair of red patent leather Mary Janes, the same kind of shiny red as these shoes. I'd begged for them, pleaded, whined. They were the most beautiful shoes in the world. But my mother had refused. "I'm going to have to buy you communion shoes later this year and I can't afford two pairs."

"Oh, I don't care! I won't make communion. I have to have those shoes."

She gave in and bought them for me. Wearing them was heaven on earth. I twirled and danced down the street in them, making little tapping noises. Every little scuff was dutifully buffed with a Kleenex at the end of every wearing, before they were returned to their original cardboard shoe box.

And then on the day of my communion, she had a white pair waiting for me, too. She was a financial genius! She must have secretly been saving for months. See? She found the money after all! She had done it because I was special and she loved me and everything turned out all right in the end, just like on TV.

But a closer look at them revealed—to my absolute, stunned horror— how she had really managed it.

She had painted over my red shoes with white polish.

My gorgeous red shoes were now prim and white. "I told you we couldn't afford two pairs," she reminded me, answering the wordless accusation written all over my stricken face.

They looked fool-proof at first, but as I walked up the church aisle the day of my communion, they began to chip.

White flakes fell behind me like so much dandruff. The shoes became slowly redder, and redder, and redder. My bowed head might have looked like piety, but it was bowed because I was riveted to the travesty overtaking my feet. By the time I reached the altar, I was an over-tall second grader receiving Holy Communion in white-flecked red shoes.

My true self: secretly disrespectful of the nuns and teachers, lazy about homework, greedy for shining red shoes, had been revealed in front of the entire congregation.

You could paint your shoes white, but you couldn't hide what you really were inside—a girl who loved red shoes—not from God. Not when you were a girl who had even been willing to forego communion just for a pair of beautiful shoes. God had heard me say that. Why did I think he wouldn't?

This memory shakes me, but I don't exactly want to cry, even though something like tears is moving around beneath my skin at the ridges of my eyes. I don't want it.

I put back the red heels. Checking outside through the plate glass window and door, I see that the heavy rain has turned to a drizzle, and I hurry out the door. I don't stop until I am in the grocery store and standing in front of the meat section.

Wow! Ambushed, after all-—by a pair of red shoes.

And then I realize something amazing, something so obviously clear I can't imagine why I haven't known it all along. It isn't the red shoes that have given me this nagging feeling that's always sort of there in the back of my mind, behind everything I do: that I'm not good enough, that other kids are somehow better, more deserving. The red shoes made me feel pretty, like dancing, like life was good and I was special. They weren't bad.

It was the *white* shoes that have done that to me—the crummy, painted-over white shoes!

My hair has gotten wet, and is dripping down my forehead. I fish in my pocket for a tissue and find some more single dollars and change, enough to pay the tax on those shoes.

We have deli ham still in the meat keeper and there is powdered creamer for my mother's coffee in the morning. The end of the week isn't that far off.

I leave the market and return to the store. The red shoes on display are just my size, like they're waiting for me, and soon they are in a bag at my side—my shoes; shoes that show the world a girl who loves bright red shoes, not little white prissy shoes. If anybody doesn't like it, who cares? Nobody is going to paint over these shoes, not ever again. I'll hurt anybody who even tries it.

As I walk home through the mist, I look up and imagine my new best friend, Chiron the Wounded Healer, wheeling around in outer space in his goofy egg-shaped orbit and probably wearing red patent leather shoes, or at least dreaming of them.

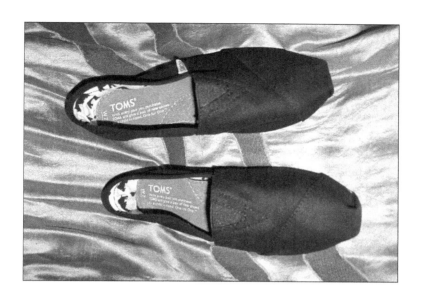

II. THE PRESENT

If the Shoe Fits, It Isn't Sexy by Karen Clark

It seems to me that women fall into two camps—those who love shoes and who own a closetful, and those who never want to wear them at all. And yet, I seem to be in the middle. Ideally, I'd like to be barefoot at all times (impractical if you live in New York, where so many dog owners are pooper-scooper scoff-laws) and yet, when we moved into a smaller apartment, I found I was reluctant to donate five or six boxes of unworn shoes to a good cause, such as the charity thrift shop. These shoes all have three-inch heels, which is why I never wear them, and they cost me a small fortune in a San Francisco shop that caters to women with extra-wide feet (that would be me) and also, of course, to female impersonators. They were bought two years before the birth of my son, who has now turned seventeen, and there is not so much as a scuff mark on the soles. That is because I only wore them to bed, when my former husband was in the mood for something that set off stockings. The shoes are far too painful to wear on the street. Not only does being jacked up on heels send shooting pains from my toe to my ankle, but my calves feel like I am being racked after about half an hour of tottering around in them. My present husband, thankfully, does not entertain a shoe fetish, and so there is no reason to hang onto the torture shoes—except that they'd cost me such a damn lot of money.

I could, of course, give them on consignment to my friend—let's call her "E"—who sells discarded finery on Ebay. But I'd have to wear them for a while and mucky them up a bit. E has made quite a killing in the worn-and-smelly, specialty-shoe-interest niche. Having discovered that there is a thriving market for ripe, stinky ladies' shoes, E has taken to turning up for lunch dates in disreputable footwear of dubious origin (she haunts all the thrift shops, and every female neighbor in her sixteen-story co-op has been begged to discard cast-off footwear at her apartment door.) Some of these shoes fit her; some of them don't. Often, she will plunk into her seat brandishing a testimonial from a satisfied customer.

"Look at this!" she hoots. "The creep says he went on a business trip without his wife and took my shoes along for company! '*I had a wonderful time—three glorious nights in a Cincinnati hotel, and the scent stayed strong and powerful all weekend! Please let me know when you'll be posting anything new. I'm especially interested in anything you may have in a beaded pump, and you know how I adored those red stilettos!*'" She throws the letter disdainfully across the table. "Perv!" Then a satisfied smile crosses her face. "You know, I paid two bucks for those, and I got him for forty-five. Wait till he gets a load of these!" She sticks her foot into the aisle and waggles her toes, nearly tripping up a waiter.

The point, I suppose, is that shoes are sexy. What I've never been able to figure out is why they're sexy. How much can you really do, sexually, with a foot? I mean, as opposed to parts of the body that are actually designed for sex? As for doing something to a foot heavily armored in a fetish shoe—ouch. Is the classic pump sexy because a guy chasing his secretary around a desk has a better chance of catching her if she's wearing a pair of high heels? And then there are boots. No argument—boots are hot. Just ask Nancy Sinatra whether she'd even think about singing a song called "These Flip-Flops Are Made for Walking."

Not all shoes are created equal. I'm not saying it makes any sense, but—it's a fact. Some shoes are sexy, others are not. I guess that's why I can't force myself to get rid of the torture shoes. Some part of me simply can't bear to throw away Sexy.

Footprints and Shoes by N. Lynne Fix

Aunt Isabelle always warned me about selecting shoes—never too tight, err on the side of comfort, and always choose a pair to grow into. According to her, you could tell much about the life and status of a man by his shoes, but even more about his soul, by the footprints he leaves behind.

While living in China, I became fascinated by the old tradition of foot-binding, and listened to scholars discuss the custom and process of "molding" the three-inch golden lotus. Starting at the age of three, the girl's feet were tightly bound with cloth strips. The toes were broken, to keep the feet from growing larger than 10 cm, or about 3.9 inches. After years of binding, the arches of the feet snapped, and the heels were mashed against the front toes, resulting in a concave arch, similar to a camel's hump.

The lotus shoe fashion gained popularity in traditional China, turning on its head the old adage "if the shoe fits, wear it." Instead, the foot was "molded" to fit the miniature shoe. It was a painful process and an odious tradition that deformed many, simultaneously stigmatizing women who kept their natural feet by characterizing them as ugly and not marriage-worthy.

Foot-binding waned in the 20th century with the end of imperial dynasties and the increasing influence of Western fashion. As the practice faded, many of the women were released from the binding, which was sometimes a more painful experience than the binding itself. Denounced by many and even outlawed by Mao in the 1950's, the foot-binding custom is a taboo subject in China today, and it is nearly impossible to find anyone who will talk about the subject, or acknowledge that it ever existed.

I pressed one of the Chinese scholars to tell me where I could find more information about the foot-binding custom, and he indicated there was a private shoe museum in another city which exhibited old flower lotus shoes. Excited to be on a fact-finding expedition, I set out the next day to visit the "secret" Lotus Shoe Museum.

I took the train and arrived in the afternoon, embarked upon my journey. Curiously, there was no mention of the museum on the Internet, in the tour guides or in any city literature. I spent a few hours asking taxi drivers, and even went to a tour office inquiring about the location of the shoe museum, but with no luck. My questions drew quizzical eyes, disinterested mutterings, and one sour respondent directed me to a nearby flower shop. After five hours I realized that I was getting nowhere, so I went to the ancient cultural street and approached an old man selling calligraphy and Cultural Revolution memorabilia in an art store.

"Is there a shoe museum near here?" I asked.

"What?" he yelled, staring at me through his oversized bifocals.

I leaned in closer, so the old man could hear my words. "I'm looking for a shoe museum, old traditional lotus shoes. Is there any shoe museum near here?" I cracked in a loud voice.

The old man looked at me, stroking his straggly white beard. "You want to buy some? Too small for you," he drawled, glancing at my size nine shoes.

"I'm visiting from Beijing and I was told there is a museum here that displays lotus shoes worn by beautiful Chinese women—you know, like your wife," I persisted.

He opened his mouth, showing yellow worn teeth, and belched. "Down the street, turn left and circle around the back. How do you know my wife?" he added, grinning, as I thanked him for his assistance.

Ten minutes later I was at the Lotus Shoe Museum, nestled in the historic old part of Tianjin. My excitement was short-lived, as I read the sign pasted on the door notifying patrons that the museum was open on Wednesdays and weekends. Disappointed but not deterred, I decided to come back later.

A few weeks later I made my way back to the Lotus Shoe Museum. I entered the lobby, waking up the attendant, who seemed very surprised to see a foreigner walking through the door, or, indeed, anyone willing to pay a fee. I passed him the ticket that I purchased at the ticket kiosk, and he steered me to the entrance.

It was a dimly lit place, with several glass displays that showed the custom of foot-binding and its history, spanning decades of shoe fashion in old China. There were shoes made of wood, clay, leather; many adorned in silk, all beautifully dyed in elegant flower motifs and so fragile that they reminded me of toddler's shoes, rather than adult footwear styled in the shape of a lotus flower.

One display case showed the scene of a wedding night, where the groom was gifted with a box of shoes and instructions on how to have sexual intercourse and foreplay with the bride, starting with massaging her stunted feet. Despite the restriction of movement and flexibility, women with bound feet were considered sexually appealing. The wobbly gait that replaced an upright stride and miniature bones were considered erotic elements, as was depicted in photos of men stroking and licking the stunted feet and deformed toes.

At the corner of the room was a large map of China, with color codes representing locations where foot-binding was predominant in its heyday. The map showed Southern China and ethnic minority regions, where foot-binding had not caught on, probably because of resistance to the imperial court and because minority women were more active in the day-to-day toil of making a living.

I departed the museum after a few hours, exhausted, but satisfied that I had visited the "secret" and unadvertised Lotus Shoe Museum. I taxied to the modern part of the city, where there were many fashion stores and outlets, and watched the shoppers steam by while I sipped my coffee, pondering the images I had just seen at the museum.

A wave of teenage boys fanned by, toting bags labeled Nike, Adidas and Li-ning. Their clothes signified they were jocks, and they moved in fits and starts up the street, jumping and spinning in the air, making baskets in imaginary hoops. Their shoe brands affirmed their enthusiasm for basketball and their hopes of following in the Yao Ming tradition.

A few minutes later I spotted a stern-faced monk wandering through the crowd, stopping long enough to ask passers-by directions. Wearing a flowing yellow robe and ill-fitting speckled glasses, he seemed unfazed by modern fashion and wore brown threadbare sandals that seemed to predate the long march. He continued on his way, disappearing into a bookstore, undeterred by modern conventions and fads, pursuing his mission of peace and harmony.

A street vendor vaulted up the street, attired in the blue uniform and dirt-smudged black boots that were standard issue for public workers. She worked in a mechanical fashion, tactfully moving through the crowds while clearing the garbage with latex-gloved hands. Her boots sealed her status as a manual worker who performed the dirty work of society, and the pulsating bands of shoppers registered her presence by avoiding contact and swarming around her as she swept up the litter-strewn street.

"Anything else?" I was startled by the café hostess, who wanted to know whether I was finished or wanted another cup of coffee. She clanked away on her fashionable, high-platform shoes, reminding me of the arched nodes of the bound feet I had seen earlier in the day.

Shoes do tell a story about an individual's lifestyle and culture, but they do not always tell us about the character of man. Aunt Isabelle was right. Shoes leave their imprint on style, culture, gender, and the financial condition of the wearer, but a man's footprint tells us about the legacy left behind.

Parts of a Life in Shoes by Lyn Di Iorio

Shoes of the Present

I am shoe-browsing online and point to a pair of shoes that beguile me: wedge ankle boots designed by CeCe Chin. The black leather is embossed all over with flowers and swirls, and jeweled with brass studs. The points and curves of the boot shapes remind me of both harem slippers and footwear worn by the Hell's Angels.

I call over my husband and ask him to take a look.

Sometimes my husband, Xavier, will share in my own fascination with an item of apparel, and will say, "It'll look great on you. You should get it."

But now he looks a little mystified. "Why do women need so many shoes?" The tone of his voice gentles from bafflement to loving indulgence.

"But I don't have that many shoes," I say, slightly puzzled. "Maybe fifteen to twenty pairs and some of those are ancient. I'm no Imelda." Now my voice is a tad defensive.

Xavier smiles fondly and looks away.

But I know what he means. He means that I—and "women" he does and doesn't know—have more shoes than we need.

Now, I don't think my husband is totally ascetic. Xavier likes to collect radios. He owns a Bakelite Fada, a stately 1930's oak Philco, a very rare black Emerson Bakelite tombstone, an even rarer old British Ekco, and many transistors from the 1940s, 1950s, 1960s, and 1970s. In his mythical past, he owned many more radios, which he sold in a fit of Zen Buddhism, but that's another story. He watches for antique radios on EBay with as much eagerness as I follow the shoe sales on Zappos.com.

When it comes to clothes and shoes, however, my husband is a Spartan. He has only four pairs of shoes; two pairs are for work, one is a pair of loafers for, well, loafing, and the third is a pair of sneakers for the gym or walking in Central Park.

I would not say that I collect shoes the way my husband collects radios. After all, I rarely forget the question of how much the shoe costs, or how much use I can get out of the shoe, even if its beauty makes it seem to float on air and not on this earth. There is absolutely no use that my husband can get out his beautiful antique radios.

I consider boots to be my preferred choice of shoe wear precisely because I find them useful, but also sexy in a streetwise way. I like them high heeled but wedge shaped and usually in buttery black leather, although sometimes I adore them in stretchy black Viscose fabrics that make me look as if I am wearing tights stitched onto wedge heels. My current favorites are a pair of three inch Biviel loose ankle boots criss-crossed in leather ties. They are very rocker chic, but also have just a hint of the gladiator sandal about them. They add height to my five foot frame; they are edgy and—egad—they are so comfortable, I hardly notice them when I wear them.

I have worn them so much in the past year and a half that I wore through the plastic in the heels, which are now lopsided. Their current state makes me think of Marilyn Monroe's trick for an attractive walk: cut a bit off the bottom of one heel, so that the ass will wiggle. But my Biviels will soon pass from the ass-wiggling mark into the ankle-breaking stage. They are dying quickly because I love them so much. I have two other pairs of boots that used to be like my Biviels, but wore out in the heel, too. One pair is tall, and has the buttoned-up look of Victorian boots—but with a wedge. I can't bring myself to throw them out, because of how much I like them, and occasionally I wear them despite the lopsided-heel issue. So I have at least four old, loyal, outworn pairs of boots like these among my shoes. Hardly ostentations.

On the other hand, I can be seduced by an impractically gorgeous concoction in patent leather, in just the same way that my husband can be seduced by a red and white Catalin radio. I have a pair of cobalt patent leather wedges that ever-so-slightly reveal the spaces between my first and second toes, as if they were breast clefts. Every time I look at the way the blue leather highlights my instep, I feel happy. The blue lights up my foot and me. I don't even remember what brand the cobalt blue shoes are. I wear them in the spring and summer and they are a big support in my wardrobe—I can wear them with just about anything. I will own these shoes even when I am in my seventies and can't wear high heels anymore.

I am hardly tempted by some of the types of shoes that are thought to be seductive. For example, there are the spindle-heeled Manolo Blahniks, made famous by Carrie Bradshaw on *Sex and the City*. The severely arched vamps of Blahnik's shoes seem to me to define both "femme" and "hourglass." They are lovely, but I can't imagine myself wearing them. I cannot wear a tall spike and perambulate at the same time. However lovely a shoe, I feel as if I would need to be able to walk at least a few paces in it. I don't really know any woman writer who wears Blahniks. On the other hand, I don't know the real-life counterpart of Carrie Bradshaw: author Candace Bushnell, presumably a woman who has New York legs—meaning they are toned by walking—and numerous pairs of Blahniks.

That is not to say that I don't covet spike heels on occasion. It has happened, at times, that a shoe's beauty made me lie to myself about its use. Take the netted "circus" sandal booties that I recently saw on the Saks Fifth Avenue online site. Medallions of black suede edged with silver leather and set atop spiked heels achieved both a winter bootie as well as a gladiator sandal effect: supremely sexy. Although a spiked heel feels like stabbing myself in the heel, and then walking with the knife blade still stalagmited into my foot, I might have bought these Christian Loboutin fantasies. If they hadn't cost thirteen hundred dollars.

So what is my preliminary response to the question of why I have more shoes than I need? I like them high and I wear them out fast. I hold onto old ones, like old friends, even if I can't wear them anymore.

For example, I still have the red shoes I bought in high school, the shoes I thought would transport me to another existence.

Shoes of the Past

Xavier and I had known each other at our high school, Academia Perpetuo Socorro in Puerto Rico, in the early 1980s. We took several classes together. One of these was Sister Olivia's pre-calculus class for the "advanced" students. Sister Olivia, an eighty-odd-year-old Irish-American nun, spent a good half of the class leading us in the singing of spiritual lyrics in English, such as "His Peace is Flowing Like a River." Because of the resulting quasi-festive atmosphere, about fifteen percent of the class was spent in open conversation while students wrote math formulas, either in answer to homework or to in-class questions, on the board. In the remaining third of the class, the students or Sister Olivia discussed the formulas on the board.

Xavier approached me once during one of the chatting sessions. He had a huge head of John Travolta hair at the time, which our mutual best friend Hermann said that he blow-dried every morning. Xavier talked so often about independence for Puerto Rico that my classmates and I called him "Albizu," a reference to Pedro Albizu Campos, Puerto Rico's Harvard-educated nationalist, martyred to his cause of independence.

At the time, I wore suede beige moccasins with my gray pleated skirt, and white cotton shirt, and gray vest; this was the uniform for girls. Boys wore gray pants and white polo shirts.

I had a sense that the gray and beige uniform was somewhat emblematic of my life.

I had a crush on Hermann. Like me, Hermann was half Puerto Rican and half "gringo." Our sensibilities and orientation towards the mainland brought us together in most ways; but to my chagrin, Hermann seemed oblivious to me as a possible romantic partner.

On another front, I studied hard, and planned to win admittance to an Ivy League college. My father, however, wanted me to go the University of Puerto Rico and live at home, so I knew I had to win enough fellowship support to get my father to agree to let me go.

I had to go. I felt a sense of suffocation in my tiny world on the island. I was locked into the sidewalk I walked from our modest apartment on calle Marti to the rigorous Catholic school I attended. Sometimes after school, I would escape to Ponce de León avenue and walk in and out of the shops, or drink *café con leche* at a *come y vete*; beyond that, I felt that there wasn't a whole lot going on in my existence except great grades, my editorship of the school newspaper, and my crush on a boy who didn't like me.

I was standing up in the chatting session in Pre-calculus, and Xavier walked over to me.

He smiled boldly, "You're pretty, but too skinny."

I remembered that one of his girlfriends, an underclassman, had come looking for him last semester at some point just as the math class was ending and we were about to take our lunch break. She had a pretty face and very dark skin. Unlike me, she had an hour-glass figure. He liked them full-bodied, so he must be making fun of me.

I decided I was vaguely insulted by his remark. I grimaced a little, and walked away.

After school, I was walking along Ponce de León avenue, thinking about how "almost-pretty" I was. It was then that I looked in the store window and saw a pair of red shoes. They were lace-up flats, but the leather was bright red, almost flame colored. Compared to my boring beige loafers with the gummy heels, these shoes had possibilities.

I walked into the store and stroked the soft leather. I looked at the name brand: Clarks. I would later learn that they were English shoes.

These were not like the red leather shoes that had danced the girl in the fairy story to death. I imagined those as an almost burgundy red, and with spiky uncomfortable heels.

These were soft, like lips. Something to kiss, and kiss me back.

I convinced my mother to buy them for me. We weren't supposed to violate the gray and beige colors of the school uniform, so I decided I would slip into the shoes right after school was over.

The red shoes, lovely English shoes, seemed to promise a world much worldlier and more sensuous than the one I lived in Puerto Rico.

The shoes made me certain that something much better for me stood in the offing beyond high school: something passionate, sensuous, and non-Puerto Rican.

The summer before college, I went on my first date; a strange outing to the beach with another half Puerto Rican, half gringo boy, who attended Robinson, the American school in the Condado. He took his tee-shirt off to reveal a body with so much hair on it that when he tried to kiss me, I squirmed away.

But I wore my buttery-soft, lipstick-red Clarks when my father and I flew to Cambridge, Massachusetts for my first year at Harvard.

Those lipstick-colored English shoes were a symbol of sorts. I would end up studying English literature at Harvard.

Wedding Shoes

More than twenty years later, Hermann, my best friend from high school, now an attorney and openly gay, called me one day—not a very common occurrence. Hermann was trying to make partner, and never had any time for socializing. He didn't have enough time, for example, for a steady boyfriend.

We chatted about the possibilities of partnership. There was a pause. "Oh, guess what," said Hermann. "Xavier is in town."

"Yeah?" I said. "Does he still have Travolta hair?"

"No, actually, his hair's thinning a little," said Hermann exultantly. Then he giggled. Not because he was pleased that Xavier's hair was thinning. Hermann doesn't have a malicious bone in his body. I could tell he was just happy about his own still ebullient head of thick, dark brown hair.

How had I not realized that Hermann was gay in high school?

"I haven't seen Xavier since high school," I said. I thought about Xavier's remark, which had bothered me so much when I was young. It wouldn't bother me now, that was for sure. I had grown out of my wallflower tendencies in my first year at Harvard, and had found a kind and nurturing boyfriend right away.

After the brunch in which we met with Hermann, Xavier and I started dating. Xavier explained that his remark from twenty odd years ago had been a come-on.

I frowned. "But you said I was too skinny."

"Anybody would know that it was a come-on. But I was trying to play it safe, too. After all, you had a mean tongue."

"I did?"

"A lot of the boys were afraid to talk to you. I only did it on a dare."

I still had those old Clarks, outsoles almost completely detached from the body of the shoe. The once bright red leather is dark and dirty from use, but I still kept them in a box in my closet.

A few months later, Xavier mentioned marriage, almost casually while he watched me ironing in my bedroom in my apartment on the Upper West Side.

I turned off the iron, and suggested he ask me formally when he was ready.

Flash forward a few months later. Xavier invited me a few weeks in advance to a 2007 New Year's party. It was going to be a sort of formal party at a wealthy Washington lawyer's house in Washington D.C., and was meant as a welcome to the governor of the state of Santa Cruz, in southern Argentina. By this time, Xavier was no longer an *independentista*. He had been associated with the Puerto Rican Statehood Party since the 1990s.

I didn't really have the right shoes.

Feeling I didn't have the right shoes really meant that I was nervous about going to a political party where there would be senators and governors and whatnot. I had never really been to an affair like this before.

Looking for the right shoes, I cruised the shoe sale section of Saks online the day before Christmas of 2006, and my heart stopped. The shoes were tall pumps with slight platforms. The heels were not as thin as spike heels. The heels—as sturdy as those of forties pumps, but much longer, and elegant in their lines—were not what riveted me. A golden and brown herringbone fabric wrapped the deeply arched vamps. Delicate scallops of chocolate patent leather edged the shoe opening. But what thrilled my heart was the delicate ornament floating over the throat of the shoe: a bouquet of tiny herringbone and brown and mustard felt flower petals. One herringbone petal had a posy of glass beads pinned to it, which glistened like tears. Fairy tale shoes, but not the red shoes that danced their beguiled wearer to death. Instead these were a pair of shoes to dance to life to, to create beauty wherever their toes tapped. Saks had reduced these Moschino masterpieces from five hundred and thirty dollars to two hundred and twenty. Over the next few days, I would go online constantly to stare at them. The day of the after-Christmas sale I bought them.

I ended up paying seventy dollars, which is the least I have ever paid for any fantasy.

I wore them to that Washington party. I could stand comfortably in them, but when I rushed out of the taxi and down the driveway to a plantation-style mansion, I felt like I was about to topple off a balcony. I tottered into the party on Xavier's steady arm, and immediately noticed a couple who looked strikingly like the deceased John Kennedy Jr. and his wife, Carolyn Bessette Kennedy.

Xavier and I walked over to meet them. They turned out to be Senator Biden's youngest son and his girlfriend. After chatting with them for a while, Xavier and I walked into a living room area, and I collapsed onto a sofa. I thought, "All right. These are not the type of shoes that are all that wearable. I'm glad I lost only seventy bucks on them."

But then those shoes found their day.

The following February of 2007, Xavier formally proposed to me on Valentine's Day. He informed me that his employer, The New York Stock Exchange—recently gone public—was changing many of its "ancient" rules by April 1st. Among other things, the Exchange was going to eliminate the traditional week of vacation given to newly married employees. Although I am a college professor and enjoy several months off a year in which I can do my writing and research, Xavier enjoyed no such luxury. That week was going to make a difference to his harried schedule.

We chose to marry in a hurry. Our small, simple ceremony, attended by my mother, Xavier's daughter Kyara, his brother José, and a few close friends, was unique.

I recalled that in high school I would never have imagined that I would marry an island Puerto Rican, certainly not anybody I had gone to high school with. Back then, I had been so intent on leaving Puerto Rico behind me.

But when Xavier and I decided to marry, part of what was so exciting was the fact that I felt that my past had come back to surprise and comfort me. I had wanted romance in high school but I had barely noticed the brash, shy, boy who tried to ask me out, despite my apparent reputation for terrible putdowns.

The second wonderful thing about our simple ceremony was that Xavier's friend, then Second Circuit Appeals Court Judge Sonia Sotomayor, married us. Xavier had been the first of all of Sonia's law clerks when she was a district court judge.

I swayed in my tall shoes, and Sonia read us the speech she had prepared for the occasion. The line I will never forget: "I want to tell you that Xavier will be an oak tree for you as he has been for me."

I knew that specifically Sonia was referring to when the Republicans stalled her elevation to the 2nd circuit court of appeals in 1998. Xavier, then head of the Puerto Rican Affairs office in Washingon, had arranged it so that ten thousand letters flooded the fax machines of members of the Senate so that she would finally get a full hearing. It was rather enthralling to hear my husband praised by this brilliant yet understated woman. Xavier assured me that she would one day become the first Puerto Rican on the Supreme Court. I believed him. My husband is no longer a brash, yet shy, boy with windswept hair and nationalist leanings. He has sliver wingtips in his hair and speaks as earnestly of Puerto Rico becoming the 51st State as he spoke, when I first met him, of the Judge's becoming a Supreme Court Justice.

Lastly, the third wonderful thing about our simple ceremony was that I found the perfect occasion for wearing my fantasy shoes. My dress was a simple, inexpensive, sleeveless, ankle-length silk white gown from J. Crew, which I had worn a few times for summer parties. I wore a short wool, marabou-feathered Tahari jacket. But it was the pumps, topped by their idylls of herringbone and felt and glass, that made me feel gorgeously decked out.

I didn't know it when I bought them, but those shoes were made for me to be married in them. I stepped lightly to my new life in them.

So why do I have more shoes than I need? Bikerish yet sleek boots march me to my fast New York pace. The pretty shoes I buy in bright colors, like the cobalt wedges, or the red Clarks of my girlhood, work symbolically. When I was in high school, the Clarks promised that I would broaden my horizons, and that I would acquire some sort of clue about how and who to date.

Some of the shoes I don't need are for walking until they fall apart; some I use to project sexiness so that I can believe in it myself. And some shoes are for dancing into life with.

Nice Shoes by Patty Nasey

My four-inch gladiator stilettos clicked unsteadily along the cement walkway toward the pool. It had only been ten minutes since I'd locked my innocent feet into their expensive black pedi-prisons but, already, a rebellion was brewing.

"Flip flops! Flip flops!" my bunions seemed to scream as they launched arrows of pain up through my toes.

I did my best to ignore them, and made my way through the clusters of well-dressed and well-heeled guests. A waiter—a white-haired man in black tie—offered me some pain relief, in the form of a glass of champagne.

"Thank you," I said, and noticed he was looking on the ground, instead of making eye contact with me.

"Nice shoes," he said, offering an unexpected yet entirely appropriate welcome to the Footwear News CEO Summit, a sort of *shoes-a-palooza* for high-level industry professionals. For the next two days, approximately two hundred Summit attendees would gather around the pool, in the bar, on the beach, at the gym or in the grand ballroom of the Four Seasons Palm Beach to talk about…shoes. From designing and manufacturing to selling and marketing to cleaning and recycling them, it would be all shoes all the time.

As Executive Director of Marketing for *Lucky* —the magazine about shopping—I had been invited to speak at the Summit. *Lucky* had recently launched an iPhone app that allowed women to shop for shoes featured in the magazine directly from their phones. The following day, my publisher would be demonstrating the app, and I would be sharing the results of a survey on women's shopping attitudes and behaviors. *Lucky*'s research had uncovered a group of recession-proof consumers we called Alpha Shoppers. Nothing could stop them from shopping and, as one young woman told us, they would go to any lengths, including eating frozen egg rolls for a week, in order to buy that pair of shoes —or handbag or jeans or jacket— that they wanted. I was thrilled to have the opportunity to share my insights with such a distinguished crowd. But I was equally, if not more, excited to wear great shoes and to meet some of the footwear royalty who would be in attendance. So I sipped my drink, tried to block out the pain and took a lap around the cocktail party.

I quickly spotted one of our advertisers, Eran Cohen, the chief marketing officer for Payless Shoe Source. He was chatting with an older, flame-haired woman who wore a black tank mini dress, spiked belt and chunky leather bracelet—definitely more East Village than Palm Beach. After Eran and I air-kissed and clinked glasses, he introduced me to his friend.

"Patty, do you know Pat? She's doing a collection for us this fall."

Oh my God, I thought, *I can't believe it's Patricia Field!!!*

Pat Field is the costume designer extraordinaire of *Sex & the City* (both the TV series and the movies) and *The Devil Wears Prada*, one of my touchstone fashion films. She also has a boutique in downtown New York City, where I bought a wig during my Dee-Lite phase in the early '90s.

"Hi," she said, extending her cocktail-ring clad hand, while giving me a not-so-subtle, shoes-to-sunglasses once-over.

As I shook Pat's hand, my eyes scanned down her trim, bare legs, finally landing on her fabulous footwear: the Dior Extreme Gladiator Platform, a $770 work of art that Sarah Jessica Parker wore throughout the first *Sex & the City* film. This shoe had famously sparked millions of Google searches, and spawned hundreds of knock-offs, including the ones I was wearing. The Diors were tough, aggressive, serious and sexy. My Calvin Klein imitations were wimpy by comparison.

"Nice shoes," I said.

The next morning, humbled by the Diors, I decided to bring out the big guns: my Azzedine Alaia denim-covered platform peep-toe sling-backs. They were originally $1,000, but I snapped them up at the annual Bergdorf Goodman shoe sale for $250. At nearly six feet tall when I wore them, I felt invincible as soon as I put them on.

The editor of *Footwear News* introduced me and I strode confidently up to the stage.

"Nice shoes," he whispered, as he handed over the microphone.

After my presentation, a shoe executive approached me to tell me how much he had enjoyed my research. "Those girls sounded like crackheads," he said. "But that's what we want."

That evening, I wore my beautiful jeweled Loeffler Randall sandals to the reception celebrating the 10th anniversary of the online shoe retailer Zappos (whose slogan is "Happiness in a Box"). On my way up to the room following the party, a man in the elevator was checking me out below the knees. I expected him to comment on my footwear, but he was apparently looking at my feet.

"You've got a serious bunion there, huh?" he said. "You should get some orthotics," he added, as he got out of the elevator. "Good night."

On the last day of the Summit, I treated my feet to a comfortably worn-in pair of Steve Madden ballet flats. I would be heading to the airport before lunch and, since my bags were packed, it was easier to just wear my flying shoes all morning.

As I was checking out, I noticed a short, balding man in a baseball cap and jeans next to me at the counter. I recognized him from his picture in the Summit program—it was Steve Madden himself. He looked over at me and, as everyone did during my stay in Palm Beach, glanced down at my feet.

"Nice shoes," he said smiling proudly, "nice shoes."

Red Sole Canvas by Missa Goehring-Plosky

"Mommy, I love your shoes. Whoa. These are so cool. They have red! I will wear them," my two-year-old, witchy-smart fashionista daughter tells me, as she examines my Louboutins for the first time. She steps into them and takes a few steps while I nervously look on, holding my tongue so I don't utter the lame mom-phrase, "Be careful." She's never walked in high heels before, but she's a natural, thanks to being a tip-toe walker since taking her first steps.

I am suddenly transported to my own childhood, galloping around our wood paneled living room in my mother's 1985 silver metallic pointy-toed shoes. I hear my grandmother's voice yelling from the kitchen, "You're going to break an ankle," as she hears the clunking pick up speed. Oh, those shoes were divine. I didn't know what sex was, but I certainly knew those shoes oozed sexy femininity. When pointy-toed pumps made a comeback in the early 2000s, I was devastated when my mother told me she had donated those shoes a few years earlier. How could she not have saved them for me?! My twenty-year-old self could've done a lot of damage gallivanting around London in those stunners during my junior year abroad, though my grandmother's prediction probably would've come true, had I teetered on the cobblestoned streets of Covent Garden, woozy from too many Red Bull Vodkas.

Baby cries cut my memories short, and I rush to put my three-month-old down for a nap. I clumsily jam my feet into my 4.5 inch black patent leather and suede Louboutins to practice walking before my toddler and I embark on a Sunday afternoon mommy/daughter dance party date.

I marvel at how much smaller our crowded one bedroom apartment feels after growing these few inches. At 5'8" and slightly taller than my high school sweetheart husband, my daily shoe is a ballet flat. Catapulted to supermodel stature, I am at my sexiest, yet the accompanying narcissism makes me feel simultaneously self-conscious. I feel statuesque, yet meek, due to my shortened stride; hyper-aware of the effort it takes to exude my usual confidence, since so much brain power is focused on maintaining stability; sweatier, as my undefined calf muscles work overdrive; and yet, they transform me into something I like.

It's been over a year since I wore these shoes, so I practice walking. I practice looking like I'm not trying too hard to look sexy. I pause to examine myself in the mirror from all angles, loving how my elongated legs look thinner than usual, and my butt appears lifted and rounder. The 8 pounds of pregnancy weight I'm still holding onto disappears into a vertical optical illusion. I practice my "these $900 shoes are NOT fake and I will NOT slouch," posture. I feel silly for lusting after myself, and for wanting to look hot on a Sunday afternoon, three months postpartum from my second child, but I push those thoughts to the back of my mind. I haven't been *out* out in ages, and these stilettos punctuate the occasion and guarantee the day's permanent etching into my memory. Some women would consider these a basic black pump, but for me, they are an occasional indulgence.

A West Village nightclub is transformed into a tot-friendly disco. I can't go out dancing with my girlfriends at 1:00 a.m. these days, so a mommy/daughter date at 1:00 p.m. on a Sunday will have to suffice. The bar is serving cocktails, wine, peanut butter-and-jelly sandwiches, pureed fruit pouches and animal crackers. Glow-in-the-dark necklaces, a disco ball, a rainbow of blinking lights and bubble machines create the ambiance in the otherwise stark music venue. My ears ring from children's squeals and the louder-than-I-expected dance music, as I sway, bounce and groove with a toddler perched on my hip, a box of organic chocolate milk in my hand replacing the cigarette-and-mojito balancing act of my twenties.

"Faster mommy, faster! Bounce me up into the sky!" Her pink patent leather Mary Janes with glitter toes get more compliments than mine, which is fine by me. I hope my shoes go unnoticed by the other parents. I didn't want to be viewed as "that mom," trying to hold onto her youth, even though that's exactly what my 31-year-old self is doing. I find it hard to believe that shoes I've owned for fewer than 5 years have seen me at both youthful abandon and responsible motherhood.

I coveted Christian Louboutin shoes for years before obtaining a pair, thinking his red soles the epitome of fashion genius, ages before they appeared on every page of every Hollywood blog. "I want to buy you a pair of those shoes you like for your birthday, but I want you to pick them out." This sentence is forever burned into my memory, as I was so excited to be offered the most extravagant gift my frugal boyfriend had ever given me. About to turn 27, I began my research into the perfect pair of shoes. A clearance rack, "quantity over quality" girl, this was the most important shoe decision I would ever make.

"I can't believe you're going to buy me thousand dollar shoes!"

"The shoes are how much?!"

"Well, I want a basic pair that won't go out of style, so those are around nine hundred dollars. Didn't you look at prices before deciding to buy a pair?"

"No. I figured they were like two, three hundred."

We had a great laugh at his oversight, and he maintained his offer of the perfect gift, so we went shopping at Saks Fifth Avenue together. My first time walking in 5 inch stilettos was on slick plush carpet surrounded by Louboutins, Jimmy Choos and Manolos. I would have looked just as graceful on the ice skating rink at Rockefeller Center. We didn't buy a pair of shoes that day. I wasn't ready to commit. I hadn't found the perfect pair.

By studying eBay listings daily, I learned that the supple leather sole, the red sole that transforms the shoe into a piece of iconic art, is easily scuffed. The color peels away at the slightest abrasion. I didn't fully believe it, until my apartment's parquet floors were enough to begin the damage. Perhaps it is this fact that makes me uniquely aware of every step I take when wearing these beauties.

It was the Fall of 2008. The subprime mortgage crisis, exposed Ponzi schemes and subsequent economic recession that devastated NYC coincided with this large purchase. As Madison Avenue boutiques were shuttering on every block, the price of luxury goods were slashed. We still had jobs, and were thrilled when I finally settled on the perfect pair of shoes that happened to be a mere $550—50% off. A relative bargain! I felt guilty for being my most excessive at a time of such hardship, but I finally had the shoes I'd always wanted, along with the same clearance shopping thrill I live for.

As the coldest winter I can remember blanketed the city in frigid darkness and moods were at their lowest, we consciously and conspicuously lived life to the fullest. I was feeling lucky to be blessed with a loving relationship and an exciting career as I emerged unscathed from my quarter-life crisis. As my company laid off half of its employees and reduced the rest of our salaries by 20%, I felt energized as part of the core team responsible for turning business around. I deserved a bit of luxury. Suddenly the playing field was level. The rich weren't so rich anymore, class lines were blurred, and our disposable income felt like it was at a premium. We put our money towards fine dining, Patron Silver, hotel stays and eventually our dream wedding.

In celebration of our 10th anniversary and the weekend we finally got engaged, we booked a hotel room at the Soho Grand for a romantic

Manhattan staycation, where the shoes made their inaugural public appearance. It snowed, and temperatures dipped into the teens, so our plans to go to a burlesque show were set aside for an evening in the comfortably plush, yet trendy and unpretentiously sexy hotel lounge.

Champagne. Top shelf. Roses. Mirrors. Mahogany. Little black dress. Lace lingerie. Thigh high stockings. Red soles. I was on fire. The shoes transformed my otherwise demure outfit into a provocative costume. Often modest, my inner exhibitionist worked in overdrive, as I put on a private burlesque-style strip tease for my fiance' that night, back in the privacy of our room, overlooking the twinkling lights of our city.

Sometimes the shoes invoke extra confidence and sassiness. Other times they help me feel like a legitimate Manhattanite in the land of Gucci, Prada, and Louis Vuitton. During a once-in-a-lifetime meal at one of Manhattan's top restaurants, Le Bernardin, where the price tag ensures an elite clientele, the shoes help me feel like I belong there. They elevate my outfit and negate the fact that we are only indulging in a $400 dinner date because the meal is a bonus for winning a marketing strategy contest at my job.

The walk to the ladies room, in between tasting menu courses, is my test. Nervously aware of my proper and posh surroundings, I am ultra-cautious not to trip or stomp ungracefully as I traverse the brightly lit dining room. On an ordinary day, I am 100% self-confident. Here, I am conscious of the paradoxical effect these shoes have on my psyche. On the one hand, I feel powerful, successful and beautiful, but also uncomfortably on display, as though I can't go unnoticed and any misstep could be critiqued by others.

Sometimes the shoes adorn my feet because I want to be on display, to look like a star, to live out the modeling fantasies I've craved since my youth. For my bachelorette party, my last hurrah before a honeymoon pregnancy would permanently reverse the rotation of my world, I surprised my bridesmaids with a high-fashion photo shoot during our weekend trip to Washington, D.C. I hired a paparazzi-style photographer, and instructed the ladies to dress to impress. For me, that meant curled locks, cat-eye liquid eyeliner, custom ivory floral headpiece, poppy red designer mini-dress, and my Louboutins.

My bathroom mirror is usually the recipient of my wannabe-model gaze, but with a photographer present, I put on my fiercest show yet. I struck pose after pose for hours, as we journeyed from my hotel suite, to the lounge, to a tongue-in-cheek trek to nearby church steps. Hand on my waist, pouty lips, eyes blazing, gams a mile long, knees angled toward one another, hip popped to maximize my curves, ankles looking particularly narrow and graceful, I consciously captured my youth. Twenty-eight looked good on me.

Now thirty-one and blistering, I find it humorous that today is actually my first time really dancing in these shoes—shoes best designed for the walk from a taxi to an entrance to a perch, the toe bed now excruciatingly narrower after two pregnancies have done irreparable damage to my feet, widening them and making me go up a half size. I chuckle to myself, between winces, as I compare my voluptuous toe-cleavage to my milk filled boobs. After a few songs, I put the shoes back in their dust bag in exchange for the nude ballet flats I wore on the subway and dance the afternoon away comfortably, able to focus on having a great time with my daughter rather than on the status of my feet.

"Did the shoes fit okay?" my husband asks that evening, recalling my concern that pregnancy had widened my feet.

"No. They felt awful. I had to take them off after a few songs. I can't wear them anymore unless I find a place to have them stretched."

"You could sell them," he adds hopefully.

"True."

But the thought of posting photos of the shoes for potential eBay buyers stops me in my tracks. I would have to post an image of their scuffed red soles, showing the wear and tear that diminishes their resale value. But that red sole is a canvas of memories, and each scuff mark represents a step, a moment in time, a version of myself. It dawns on me: The scuffed Louboutin sole is not a defect. It is a visual portrayal of adventure, of distance traveled, of place and time, of my relationship between fashion and identity.

Actually, I can never sell them. I will save them and the stories they conjure up for my daughters.

Maud Frizon's Dream by Victoria A. Chevalier

"You Ain't Living Till You've Had a Pair of Mauds…"

The duffel bag was a relic from the 1980's, one of those cheap, plastic affairs with a pleather lining. But it had wheels, and a handle (one of the first of its kind, I am sure); upon further inspection it was clear that despite some wear and tear it, too, had managed to survive. I unzipped the long zipper at the bag's top and a rainbow popped out in the darkness of the attic closet. It was an old Ecuadoran throw from my undergrad years, magnificent in magenta, orange, and purple. Another throw of darker hue peeped out from under the first, and I remembered how I had left them here in 1994, right before leaving for Cornell's graduate program in English. They were the sort of items one thinks one has no use for when one is moving on to a wonderfully exciting and magnificent life. I was charmed not only with the memory of curling under these throws at night after long hours of undergrad study all those years ago, but also at the memory of their greeting me with riotous color in my Washington Heights apartment every day before I left for school.

As I pulled both of the throws out of the bag, it planked to the floor, and I realized something else was hidden at the bottom. Inside a plastic bag, discreetly folded underneath the Ecuadoran throws, a pair of thigh-high boots slept, also discreetly folded against the years.

These were the most magnificent pair of footwear I had ever owned in the 1980's, my decade of decadence and escape from the reality of my history, and my identity. This decade was also almost the destruction of my future, and these Maud Frizon pirate boots had seen it all from the vantage point of many a New York City street.

I could not believe that I had ever owned anything so lush, so beautifully handcrafted, and so ostensibly frivolous. My life as a "non-traditional" undergrad student, and then as a full-fledged Ph.d. allowed me to become the person I felt I was always meant to be: a fully qualified University professor, a serious person, an intellectual, yet these boots spoke to another part of my identity which I had relentlessly buried upon return to college in the early 1990's. In these chocolate brown suede Captain Morgan's with the intricate black lace overlay was woven my stoic, college-educated rejection of the frivolities of fashion, itself a thin slip that barely covered the pleasures of the exquisitely clothed body. I could theorize about style and fashionable taste in the polytechnic for intellectuals at my elite graduate school program, but I could not occupy my own body in those halls in the way I did in the 1980's in these boots. There in the hallways of Goldwin Smith it was verboten to have a body, let alone to enjoy it. No Lolitas were allowed there, unless they existed in the pages of Vladimir Nabokov's novel.

As I slipped them on I remembered how supple the leather lining was, as it once again greeted my foot, my ankle, my calf, and my knee. Silkier than butter was what that lining felt like. The lace on the toe of the left boot had worn away a bit, exposing the suede to the weather, but the toe itself was still exquisitely shaped. This was not a witchy toe over a kitten-heel like so many of the Manolo Blahniks and Maud Frizons sported by Eastside debutantes and the Ellen Barkins of that era. This toe looked like it could easily climb a pirate ship's Brigadoon mast in style. Turning down the cuff exposed more of the soft, milk-chocolate suede; there was a spot on the right cuff that looked like a dot of oil, but otherwise, they were perfect. I obviously had them resoled before storing them away, and the flat, black rubber shined in the mirror as if it were recently polished with a caring hand.

This footwear had girded me against life in the 1980's in New York City when I skipped from job to job while making money as a fit-model. I would never be a supermodel, or even a catalog model; even had I not lacked the height for it, my teeth were impossible for an image-factory that insisted only perfection, if not character, existed. But my body was a perfect size 2, or 4, depending upon diet and workouts; and for that, 7th Avenue loved me.

During that time, I met stylists, and photographers, and other girls like me—"exotic" girls now accepted into the fashion industry—to a point: Latina, African American, West Indian, Asian girls, all of us trying to make it through the fashion world, the club scene, and Madison Avenue with little experience, a lot of courage, sometimes a healthy destructiveness, and a great drive to live life by escaping our respective origins. Most of us were from the boroughs, and had grown up on pasteurized images of beauty and style like Suzanne Somers, and Heather Locklear. Despite our much desired darker tones, however, we, too, were imperfect of feature, height, weight, or talent. Our impossibilities never seemed concrete enough for us to take seriously, yet during that time these boots helped me whittle away at the illusions that I would ever be anything more than an imperfect face attached to a perfectly-sized "for-fittings-only" body.

I must have stored them away around 1992. This was the year the 1980's truly ended in terms of fashion: big hair, huge shoulder pads, and neon-colors worn by people masquerading as adults were definitely on the way out by the time Bill Clinton was elected President. It was also the year I knew I would pursue at all costs a Ph.d. in English, to truly escape a good deal of what I then considered too painful about my black and working-class origins. It was around this time that Doc-Martens became my battleground footwear. I stomped through the halls of academia in those cherry-red, steel-toes, inhaling Kant's *Third Critique*, bildungsroman novels, and feminist theory the way an addict inhales the last bit of hashish in a pipe. That stomp substituted for the gliding ease with which I walked Madison Avenue in the 1980's in my Maud Frizon's. Despite my working-class background, and despite my race, that stomp indicated a sense of power I felt I could exert upon the halls of academia, in a way I could never shake-up the whitewashed, monochromatic fashion industry.

Different journeys and different battlegrounds require different footwear. As I pirouetted in the mirror of the attic of the home that my parents built for us, I knew I would wear them again. After all, the 1980's had returned to the fashion scene with a vengeance. 2008 was all about the skinny jean, blouson tops, and pirate boots; what could be more 1980's than that? Living in these Mauds had gotten me through that decade, and my deliberate forgetting of them probably buttressed my survival of the 1990's, graduate school, and the early "aughts." But if a girl cannot read the modernists and live in her body while wearing gorgeous footwear, what was the point of all that battle, of all that survival?

I turned the toe of my right foot out to better see the delicate arch of the boot. Then I packed away the throws, gathered the duffel in my arms, and climbed down the stairs girded in a Maud Frizon dream, moving forward toward the fashionability of living.

Patent Pointed Pump, Pink by Doris Barkin

I am staring into my iPhone 4, eyes glazed from overuse. I squint; my eyes narrow. I struggle to sharpen my vision. There it is, displayed on my lavender tinted Bergdorf-Goodman Shoe App. A nano-sized, digital image, which I cannot resist. I feel my heart accelerate. Though my eyes are already burning and blurry, I must goggle at the perfection of Patent Pointed Pump, Pink.

This shoe is a cathedral: pointed arched vault supported by a gleaming four and a half inch heel colonette. A creamy-bright-pink architectural dream. However, this edifice is decidedly un-ecclesiastical; this shoe is the ultimate in seduction. It is Eros incarnate. It is a cross between Frederick's of Hollywood and haute classical elegance. I want the shoe in my phone to come alive. I want to slip it onto my curved foot on my elongated leg. Not like Cinderella. Like Hedy Lamarr. My fairy tale heroine is a vamp.

Vamp. The front part of a shoe. Vamp. A woman who uses sexual attraction to exploit men. I am meditating on the connection. The relationship between women's shoes and men is a conundrum. Why are shoes fetishized? I think back to my own fixations: where do they come from? Why do I feel powerful in my shiny, black leather to-the-knee stiletto boots? Why are my white and blue silk twill sandal pumps downright celestial? Why am I obsessed? Why am I in love?

I am awash in memories of shoes. At eleven I was desperate for white Go-Go boots, the ones I saw in the teen magazines; the ones that the straight-haired, long-banged Mods wore with their mini-skirts on Carnaby Street, hanging out with the Beatles. My girlfriends in school had them. Roberta had a pair actually, literally from London. They were divine, not fake leather like the other girls' imitations. These were plush—soft and tough at the same time. I needed them. My father, unbending, would not allow me to have them. Instead, my father commanded me to wear a pair of shiny, emetic colored coral, square-toed, black rubber-soled buckle shoes sent by a family friend as a gift for me. I wouldn't be caught dead in those hideous things. The look of them made me ill. My father, tyrannical, booming, towering over me, yelled in his fearsome voice that I was not to leave the house unless I was wearing those hateful shoes. I cried, I begged, I pleaded.

At twenty-three, I am sitting on my parents' living room couch, visiting. I no longer live with them. I am on my own. I live with a roommate in a tiny, dingy—"charming" in real estate speak—apartment in Greenwich Village. I can barely afford cleaning supplies to mop the miniature bathroom and kitchen. Fantastik is a luxury item. I am swinging my crossed legs, arguing politics, discussing teachers' labor union benefits, half-child, half-adult. My father peers at my shoes. He leans over to feel the bottom of the worn-out sole. He asks, hesitatingly, if I would like him to bring the shoes to his shoemaker to have them fixed. It becomes a ritual. He shows up at my apartment with a brown-paper bag. Stuffed inside are my shoes: shined, spiffy, brand-new. He pays, of course, and I am grateful.

At eight years of age, my job is to shine my father's shoes. I love this job. He brings out his tools: shoeshine box, horsehair brush, Kiwi cake polish, cloth rag. He hands me his black brogues, from Florsheim on Thirty-fourth Street. Daddy is meticulous about his shoes. He instructs me to first rub off any dirt, then put my whole little fist inside the shoe, apply the thick, black polish all over the shoe with the other hand, then buff and shine with the rag. I feel responsible, given a very important task.

Over the years, as I grow into a woman, I observe that my father marvels at the high heels I show up in. Higher and higher, I risk toppling, yet I make my voyage from Manhattan to Queens on buses and trains in clicking high heels.

"Can you really walk in those shoes?"

"Oh, yes, they're really comfortable," I lie.

"Azoy."

My father reads *The New York Times* religiously. He wants to show me an Op-Ed piece on Balkanization and the collapse of Yugoslavia. He thumbs through the first few pages of the *Times*, crowded with ads from Cartier, Rolex, Saks Fifth Avenue. He points to Manolo Blahnik Satin Pumps, eight hundred sixty-five dollars. He is wide-eyed.

"They don't know *what* to charge anymore. Meshiggeh."

I am in a reverie of distant images. I recall the trip to Poland with my brother and father. My father hadn't been back since 1939 when, with hundreds, he sleepwalked from Warsaw through the night, eventually crossing over the border into Russia. We have come to reclaim, in a way, but it is difficult, dare I say, impossible to reclaim what is lost and destroyed forever. We take a trip to Auschwitz, where my mother had been interned; it has now been converted into a museum. I walk with my father, wordlessly, alongside huge glass cases of valises, artificial limbs and orthopedic devices, and human hair. The case that fills me with the most horror is the one that is over-filled, from bottom to ceiling, with shoes. It seems to contain all twelve million shoes worn by those who perished or were gassed. Shoes piled on shoes. Most of the shoes are dusty, grimy, worn leather work-shoes, or canvas lace shoes. But amid them are red leather ladies' heels, and dainty strap wedges. I linger, scrutinizing each one, agape, but silent.

It is a lost world. In my world, I am encased in the fantasy of Patent Pointed Pump, Pink. What would it be like to own those shoes and slither into them? A last image is crowding me. My father and I prance around the room. He is leading me. He tells me to place my little feet on top of his big shoes, and we prance around the room. I am almost as tall as he is. He is carrying me. I am giddy, lifted high, dancing.

Boy-Wannabe Shoes by Maia Wynne Kallen

When we were eight years old, my best friend Emma and I transitioned out of our fairy tale princess phase and entered our tomboy, or as we called it, "boy-wannabe" phase. Everything we said or did had to be boy-approved; we had short hair, dressed in baggy clothing, wore baseball caps, and hung out with our boy pals. But above all of our boyish characteristics, the most defining was our matching pairs of red Converse high-top sneakers.

As boy-wannabes, Emma and I looked to Wayne and Garth from *Wayne's World* as our role models. For me, Wayne was the epitome of cool. I was eager to get authentic-looking holes in my jeans, but I knew that merely cutting holes wouldn't do the trick; it would look like I was trying too hard. I spent classroom free time dragging my knees on a carpet in order to achieve the look I so desperately wanted, ignoring the strange looks I received from my teachers. A rugged look to my Chucks was no less important, so I roughed up my sneakers until they fell apart: for *Wayne's World* purposes, it was necessary to have a worn-out pair of Converse. Anything clean or new-looking would have been a disgrace.

These shoes became my everyday companions. Something about the high-tops and the famous "All-Star" badge at the inner ankle made me feel genuine, and all the more like a boy.

Sixteen years have passed and I am 24. My younger sister, Chloe and I decide that we will make this year's Halloween an event to remember. She suggests that we dress up as Wayne and Garth. I, who still have the long black hair and have perfected his mannerisms, will be Wayne; and Chloe, who wears glasses and can truly capture the awkwardness of Wayne's sidekick, will be the classically awkward Garth. As I plan my costume, I realize that I will need to buy a new pair of Converse. Imagining myself wearing them as an adult feels strange. Can I successfully retreat to my long-ago, essentially retired, boy-wannabe days?

Two weeks before Halloween, I go into a small shoe store in Soho to obtain this vital part of my costume. Immediately, excuses as to why I shouldn't buy the sneakers come to mind. I notice their inflated price, and hesitate to pay fifty dollars for a pair of shoes that used to cost my mother fifteen; I don't like conforming to popular trends and every teenager walking down the street seems to own a pair of these sneakers, yet I decide to toss my ambivalence aside, and wriggle my feet into a brand-new pair of black Converse low-tops.

I look in the mirror, seemingly back at my eight-year-old self, and I wonder: am I too old to be wearing these sneakers? Ambivalence sets in again, but I walk around for a few minutes to make sure the size is right and, before I know it, I fall in love with them. I walk out of the store thinking that I have just spent the best fifty dollars of my life. I bring the shoes home and show them to Chloe. With an intent frown, she tells me it is important that I scuff them up so as to be prepared for Halloween. She asks me if she can step on the pristine white semicircles covering my toes, but I insist that any wear and tear must occur naturally, for the sake of authenticity.

As the day approaches, I buy a pair of worn-out jeans at a thrift store. This time, I save myself the embarrassment of dragging my knees on a carpet; instead, I cut holes at the knees before putting my jeans through the wash in order to give them just the right "distressed" look.

Halloween is a triumph. Both Chloe and I revel in our achievement of coolness; she, with her more-than-worn-out red Chucks, and I with my not-as-worn-out (but good enough) black ones.

Since buying the sneakers, formerly intended only for my Halloween costume, I have worn them almost every day. They look great with every outfit I own, and have molded perfectly to my feet. And, while they may have become a current trend, at least I know that my relationship with these shoes is personal and goes way back to the old days of Wayne's World, when they were cheap and intended for basketball players. *After all*, I tell myself, *it isn't retro if you wore it the first time around.*

Sharps by Diane Goettel

Hand jobs in the den, monsters on the television screen. Blow jobs in empty houses, parents on errands. His hands under my shirt. His hands on my ass. His hands in my hair. His hands in my pants. Kissing. Kissing with tongue. Nibbled ear lobes. Tongues on necks. Creaming our jeans. Licking sweat off our lips. The scrape of first stubble. I can still smell him. I can still taste him.

I started loving Charles when I was thirteen, the year I got my first pair of heels, the year I had my first orgasm. Loving and practicing. The orgasm and the shoe—two of the first and most defining tools that I've come to use in my craft of being a woman. But it wasn't just the shoes themselves, it was the way I learned to wear them. My mother, a professional in the fashion industry, toted me to shows when I was as young as five. As we sat eye-level with the feet of those beautiful women, she coached me. "That one," she'd say, pointing to the one model who had a bit of a wiggle in her rump, "she's got a swing on her back porch." And about the one who had a spring in her step, she'd say, "There's a jig in those feet. Isn't she lovely?" So I began practicing at an early age. In Mom's shoes, at home, long before I got my very own pair of heels. When I slid into that first pair for the first time, my very own pumps, I already knew how to swing, how to jig. And men two times my age noticed, three times. I loved it. A new tool. And I sharpened it on Charles, loving him, a completed selfish act.

On the couch. Straddling his lap. Guiding his mouth to my neck. Grinding against the pressure in his pants, hard as fired carbon. Years later I'd watch a documentary about sex toys made out of Pyrex and I'd think of those nights, always half listening for movements in the hallways, always convinced that we had our parents so fooled, that they really thought that we were on other ends of the sofa, a bowl of snacks between us, just as they'd left us. Carbon in a kiln. Carbon thousands of feet below us, reaching up through that couch and blooming under his zipper, hot and about to split and spill. Hard as a diamond in a snowstorm, in a blizzard, in the Antarctic.

Charles and I dated for two years in high school, an eternity then. We were as married as you can be at that age without being in a cult. There was a time when I could replay in my mind each and every one of our sexual encounters. There was a new one each weekend. By the time I was preparing for the SATs I had hours of mental tape to replay each night. That's how I went to sleep many, many nights, wearing through the tape, everything worn down to the smallest detail, worn and worn and worn. It's no wonder I loved him so much; it was a process of self-hypnosis. Every night: his mouth in my hair, his arms around me, hands on my back, his boxers full of cum, he'd tell me he loved me. That and everything else, worn and worn.

That first pair of heels was bought for me for my first school dance, which was also the first dance that I attended with Charles. It started then. Dancing together, stiffly.

There were many dresses, many pairs of shoes. A white velvet dress for the February dance, worn with black heels. A black dress with red piping. Red heels, of course. Heels for dinner out, playing at adulthood. Followed by minutes alone in his van, as long as we could get away with, we thought, without arousing suspicion. Heels to go to the movies. Heels for concerts. I loved looking like a woman, feeling like a woman. And it was a feeling that started at the feet—ankles lifted three or more inches off of the ground—and radiated up through my bones, my skin, gaining power in my pelvis, more at the solar plexus, a burst at the breasts and another at the throat, and up and out. And I felt so like a woman with those extra inches, the arch in the foot, the pointed toe.

But it ended. It had to. It was time for college, and as Charles was a year ahead of me in school, he left first. He stayed in our hometown for school, but I knew he was going, gone, on another planet, a plane of adulthood that I couldn't access yet. And so I broke up with him before he could break up with me. It was a mean thing to do. Meaner yet, I took up with another boy, Aaron, less than a week later. I thought there was a better chance that Aaron would stick around. But I was wrong. And eventually, I left too. At seventeen. Away from home, at college, in New York, I gathered more tools, tools as powerful as the orgasm and the shoe.

Charles must have been as hypnotized as I was. There was a period in my life, after I broke up with him and before I married someone else, when we couldn't seem to stay away from each other. We lived in different cities, went to different schools, didn't even have any of the same friends any more, but there was a rhythmic reconnection. Every two years or so. We'd find each other. And, as I once said to him, "We've never been friends, certainly not *just* friends." So we'd pretend for a little while that we were just checking in. But we'd find ourselves naked. We'd meet for a drink and have the first at the bar and the fifth in bed, sheets ripped away, the clothes as well.

And there we'd be again. Naked. Hips to hips. His apartment in Pittsburgh or my apartment in New York. Sometimes, depending on the circumstances, one of our parents' houses. "Just for kicks," I'd say to myself. But I knew that we were trying to connect to those hours, those years of muffled moans and whispers and the glow of the family television. Mouths everywhere. His fingers under all of my various straps: bra, thong, sandal. Taking it all off. One time he compared me to the other women he'd slept with, his encounters in the interim between our connections. And I was surprisingly untroubled. Which made me wonder if I loved him. Not in love, I decided, just hypnotized. One finger inside. Slipped under. Two. A mouth to follow. Three. Our bodies blue, flickered across with cartoons on mute, our bodies opened up.

I worked over men with the skills that I honed at Charles' expense. There were many men in New York. And far more pairs of shoes. There was actually a time when I identified men that I slept with according to the shoes that I wore while we were dating. There was Tavio and the yellow wedge shoes, Kingsley and the olive drab alligator pumps, Boris and the tall leather boots. Heeled cowboy boots and Nathan.

The shoes and the workings of womanhood, the performance that I began to learn at five under the catwalk, that I slipped into along with my first pair of heels. It was empowering, sometimes made me terrible, but so instructive. Sometimes I think of Charles as a primer. Something that had to be returned to a few times after the first lesson had concluded, just as a refresher, to remember a few of the fine points, the memory of which may have dulled a bit over time.

One of my best girlfriends grew up with a mother who did not give her lessons in womanhood. "She shopped at Land's End," she said to me once, by way of explanation. And I hurt her feelings once, saying, "There's nothing worse than a woman wearing a great pair of heels who has no idea how to walk in them." But she loved me and forgave me and allowed me to give her lessons. "Here is how you do a jig. Move like this, and—there! there, you're really getting it!—now you've got a swing on your back porch."

Heels or not, she had a tool kit that rivaled mine. And though she may have only worn what I called "training heels" (two inches or less), her number of sexual conquests doubled mine, tripled. She knew all about hypnosis.

Training heels. Training wheels. Cutting your teeth. Getting your feet wet. Being a little green. Charles. I think it ended with Charles when we were finally practiced enough. And it was no longer instructive. It was just sex. We still may have been a little hypnotized. We may be still. I haven't seen him in years. The last time I saw him, I was walking out the back door of his apartment, heels clicking on the linoleum hallway. It was January, but he saw me off in just his boxers. We both sort of shrugged as we said goodbye and said empty words about seeing each other again the next time I was in town. But by that time, the next time, I'd found the man I was going to marry, a man who considers me to be a kind woman.

There was a moment when I realized exactly what we were doing, Charles and I, with clarity, with painful lucidity. It was during college, a summer between years. My father was moving to a new house and I was packing up my bedroom. Charles came over and noticed a pair of boots slouched in a corner, waiting to be tossed into a cardboard box. I'd purchased the boots—thigh high, dusky red leather, zippered, platforms, six inch heels—at a strip mall near my college campus, egged on by my girlfriends. They were part of a costume I was assembling for a school dance. This dance had a theme. Unlike the themes of those high school dances—Egyptian Nights, the Snow Ball—this dance was arranged around the aesthetic and practices of sadomasochism. The boots were perfect, and they were on sale.

So Charles noticed the boots and, a few minutes later I was standing in front of him, wearing nothing but the red leather. I caught a glimpse of myself in the mirror and realized, in that moment, that while I was the very picture of fantasy, I was also rather unlovely. Charles, diamond hard in his pants, said that he liked everything about the heels except for the fact that they made me an inch taller than him. He asked me to lie down, but to keep the boots on—my plan from the beginning. That was when the retrospection began, the understanding of tools and practice and performance. It was some of the most informative, most devastating sex I've ever had. It wasn't the last time that we coupled. Not by a long shot. But after that, I had a better understanding of exactly what we were doing. And it's been one of my most closely held hopes that, since then, I've learned how to be a bit kinder with the sharp blades of womanhood.

Some women, when they go through a major change in their lives, change their hair. I change my shoes. For example, on the occasion of a breakup a few years ago, I threw away all of the shoes that the man had bought for me, even though some of them where the most expensive, most beautiful shoes I owned. I think it started with those red hooker boots. After Charles left that day, that day when everything between us became so clear to me, I put them in the garbage instead of packing the up in a box, pressing them into a full can and then dragging the whole thing out to the curb.

Note: Names have been changed to protect those who gave up their innocence. So willingly.

Namibian Shoes by Samantha Reiser

I remember the exact outfit I was wearing on the eve of my arrival in Ondangwa. While the seven-hour drive through the country's landscape remains a visual hurdle, and the distinct intonations of my driver's voice are unimaginable, the pants, shirt and shoes I was wearing at the moment I walked into my *meme's* house—an entrance greeted by her infamous cries of "my baby" (an expression that would gain an almost tactile audibility throughout my two month stay) are the items that remain memorable. In many ways, this outfit—but most of all, those shoes—would prove to be significant. Forewarned that I would be a visual anomaly on the sandy roads of my town, I was ever cognizant of first impressions throughout my time in Namibia, endeavoring to understand the impact of my wardrobe upon the eyes of a different culture. While the clothes I wore that night were soon to be replaced by my more appropriate "teacher clothes," the shoes were not.

The story behind the black peep-toed flats is brisk in background, though great in meaning. Having embarked upon a cheap-clothes shopping spree the week before my departure, I had deliberately chosen the inexpensive, yet stylish flats, in an effort to retain some sense of fashion. The shoes were my last vestiges of urban New York life—a reminder, amidst the contents of my homely and untailored closet, of where I was coming from and where I was going. Little did I know that this last-minute purchase would become a seamless part of my identity that summer.

The evolution of the significance of the shoes quickly began. Arriving in Ondangwa, I found myself unwilling, almost unable, to slip them off of my feet. I'll be the first to admit their inappropriateness for the climate. The layer of white sand covering the entire town would slip in between my toes, creating a discomfort that was heightened by the pebbles that liked to follow suit. The effect of said sand on the shoes' color was vast. Their austere black was dulled daily, a color change I attempted to counteract every three days by bathing them in soapy water and scrubbing as hard as I could. The shoes quickly grew worn, with holes appearing at the bottom of the soles. And yet, although I had brought four other pairs of shoes—hiking boots, sneakers, Toms, and flip-flops— the flats remained the only ones I ever wore. My unwillingness to vary my foot's wardrobe proved counterproductive many a time. Within the camping grounds of Etosha National Park, and within the rocky hills of Raucana Falls, the shoes worked against me. My resulting stubbed toes and slow walking pace left my fellow volunteers begging me to switch shoes. This call for a change was seconded in the classroom, where my students, intrigued by my American fashion sense, begged to see more of my foot's wardrobe. Still, I wouldn't give it to them, couldn't give it to them. Day in and day out, the shoes stayed on me, weaving themselves into my self-construction, and finally coming off only after I'd landed back in New York.

I never solved the mystery of the black peep-toed flats. Why I loved them so much, I couldn't say. Maybe it was the familiar comfort they offered amidst uncharted territory; maybe it was the sleekness I felt when I put them on, a buffer to my otherwise careless aesthetic. Maybe it was just part of the unspoken law of shoes—*they* wear *you*. Whatever it was, the flats lost their identity as shoes that summer and became a piece of a much larger story.

The day before I returned to school, I embarked on yet another shopping spree, this time with an eye less toward "cheap" and more in the direction of "fashion-inspired." Walking through the aisles of a department store, I came across my Namibia shoes. I bought them at once, this second pair, meaning to replace the hole-filled, sand-colored ones of the summer. And yet, though I am wearing this newer, sleeker pair as I type this story, the original shoes are waiting for me in the closet of my college dorm. No longer wearable, they have followed me to Boston. There they remain, statuary on my shoe rack, a quiet homage to my Namibian roads.

Size 4 Construction Boots—A Talisman
on the Road to Freedom by Lisa S. Coico

Everybody has a talisman of some sort. Some people carry a lucky item in their pockets (like a four leaf clover). Others wear a certain color shirt or dress every time they have an important event to participate in. These talismans can hold great meaning for an individual. Whether it's a rabbit's foot on a keychain, a cross worn around the neck, or a lucky pair of socks, talismans are meant to bring good luck and ward off evil. For me, perhaps the most important, albeit unusual, talisman in my life was a pair of boys' size 4 orange construction boots. Though I bought them for hiking in upstate New York, those boots that I wore the summer of my junior year of college were so much more than just a pair of hiking boots. That was the summer that I broke away from my stereotypical self and learned that self-reliance and moving forward could occur one step at time.

It was a sweltering summer with little air conditioning in 1975. There was a general malaise in Brooklyn as usually accompanies the dog days of summer. I had been dating the same person since my senior year in high school—a college dropout and a construction worker. At 6'3" tall with curly black hair and the bluest eyes you ever saw, I assumed that he was "the one"—my husband-to-be, who would give me the house, the white picket fence and four children. I knew that he had a temper, which sometimes flashed out in unusual circumstances. He was very jealous, and was a boy from my neighborhood with little ambition beyond making a decent living so that he could someday afford his own house. There was nothing wrong with this dream—except it was unusual that he was paired with me, a straight-A student who loved college and longed to become a scientist one day.

Sam was jealous, but not of other men. He was jealous of my ambition. The more independent I became, the more controlling he became. By the time I reached my junior year in college, I had little confidence in myself. I knew that I was a good student and my intelligence had always brought me along. No, my lack of confidence stemmed from believing that I didn't really belong in the role of budding scientist, but that I should be thinking more about engagement, marriage and family. It was a source of constant dynamic tension. The summer of '75, however, was a pivotal point in my life, after which I never looked back, and it all revolved around a pair of boys' size 4 orange construction boots.

That was the summer that I chose to enroll in a field botany course that required that we hike several hours per week collecting field specimens and analyzing them in the laboratory. We slogged through bogs in the Pine Barrens; we hiked in Bear Mountain and in the woods of Pennsylvania. Now, I must contextualize this experience. I was a city girl, born and raised in Brooklyn. Most of my other family vacations, even those I considered exotic, such as in Europe, were completely city-based. I wandered through the streets and museums of many great cities, but never once hiked or camped outside of my own basement or backyard. I owned high-heeled shoes for dress, earth shoes for jeans, and huaraches for the summer. I had sneakers, but they were the light canvas type of Keds, which were not very useful for hiking in difficult terrain.

I needed the right shoes for the summer, but what to do? I had very small feet (women's size 4 ½) and there were simply no shoes that could fit the bill. I finally turned to an army-navy store where I discovered my talisman-to-be: Boys' construction boots. What an epiphany! It was a revelation to be able to put on a pair of boys' shoes—shoes that would normally be forbidden to me, but for this summer would be acceptable footwear for a 5', slim brunette with short, chunky-cut hair. I bought those boots and carried them home so excitedly. The first thing I did when I got home was to put them on to show Sam. Remember, Sam was a construction worker, and his size 12 steel-toed construction boots were part of his stock-in-trade. When I showed him my shoes, I was taken aback by his condescending laugh. He thought they were hilarious, and simply could not stop chuckling about how ridiculous they were. They weren't the "real thing," and never would be. They were simply boys' play shoes that imitated the real construction boots worn by real men like him.

I couldn't get his put down out of my mind. From that day forward, those orange construction boots became part of my uniform and a talisman of lucky things to come. I hiked and slogged through mud. I climbed hills and wandered along streambeds. In each and every instance, those boots were my friends. They called me to do greater things and to go beyond my comfort zone. I simply loved them more than any other pair of shoes I had ever owned, including my first Mary Janes, my first high heels and my beautiful white First Communion shoes. As the summer wore on, those boots became comfortable companions. I began to realize that my life was more than just who I would become as a wife and mother. The boots gave me freedom to walk forward sure-footedly into a different world, a world where my dreams of being a scientist could exist and where no one would expect me to conform to feminine ideals.

Although the feminist movement had begun years before, it was those construction boots that allowed me to embrace feminism and to find the masculine part of my soul. As the summer came to an end and my class decided to hold an end-of-semester party to celebrate our accomplishments, the boots became my path to freedom from Sam. Unable to see me going forward, Sam gave me an ultimatum: If I attended the party, he would break up with me. Undeterred, I donned my orange boots and marched out of my house to a new era, an era unfettered by a man who could not accept that I wanted something more from life than being a wife and mother. It was time to embrace myself for who I chose to be. Like a lucky charm, those boys' size 4 orange construction boots became my talisman. They were my lucky shoes, because they freed me to be myself and to embrace all of my heart and soul, not just the parts that played to someone else's wishes. I kept those boots for many years, as a reminder of that day, so many years before, when I chose freedom of expression over oppression.

Today is New Years Day 2012, a time for new beginnings. How far I've come since the summer of '75. Since that summer, I have discovered many new facets of myself. I fulfilled my dream of becoming a scientist, found a loving partner and had two wonderful children. I learned that juggling career and family can be an incredible challenge, but it can be done successfully. I did not have to sacrifice my personal life on the altar of my career. I have also found new dreams and passions for assisting college students in their individual quests to find their own voices and directions in life. From my current seat as President of The City College of New York, I look back and wonder how my life would have been different had I not found my talisman, those simple construction boots that gave me the courage to step boldly and unafraid into a new future. I will be forever grateful to those old boots. I hope that each and every person finds their own "pair of shoes" that guides them to a path of freedom and self-choice. We all need to forge a way of listening to our own inner voice, which knows no limits and bounds, but is creative and always seeking greater happiness and harmony.

Desert Boots by Katherine Schifani

She buys me in December, because they tell her she needs to take two pairs of tan boots to Iraq. Normally, they give them out, but they don't have her size, so they give her one pair of 7.5 wide and one pair of 8.5. I am tan, canvas, suede and a size 8. I see snow for the first time in New Jersey, where they teach her how to fire guns and apply tourniquets. Hot brass falls, bounces off my composite material safety-toe, and melts itself deeper into the snowpack.

She wears me for 44 hours in a row while we make four stops on our way to our new home. When we finally get there, she writes B POS / PCN, her blood type and drug allergy, on the side of my soles with a Sharpie, in case a bomb separates me from the rest of her body with her feet still inside. When we meet the Iraqis she lives and works with, I do my best to keep the smell of cigarette smoke from impregnating my fabric, but it doesn't work and we have to walk outside in small circles around our concrete walled compound to get the smell out.

When it rains, the mud sticks to me. It sticks, and it doesn't come off. I know when it rains now, because she wears the 7.5 wides and I have to stay under the metal bedframe until the mud dries up.

She talks to me sometimes when she cleans her guns. Usually it's because the internet here doesn't work, or because it's an odd hour back in America. She talks to me because she doesn't have anyone else to talk to, and I can tell what she needs is just someone to hear her.

Her mom sends a pair of orange plastic insoles that she shoves in under my cushions. I tried, but I couldn't support her enough on my own under the weight of ceramic plates, grenades, nine-line checklists and 285 rounds of extra ammunition. I like my orange augmentation, because we run sometimes, even with all that weight. We run to the truck, where two people have been cut in half and another has been reduced by a third by a flying piece of copper. She pulls a soldier out of a truck, sets him on the ground, yells at other people, and puts her hand on his forehead. I try not to soak up too much of him, but it's getting harder to avoid as he spreads out more and more on the blacktop below me.

When we run to helicopters, little particles of dust jump off the ground and shoot through me and I can't keep them out. I would tell her I'm sorry that I can't stop the dust, but she knows it without my saying so.

By now, I have sweat rings that turn my tan suede brown, and on my left side is a stain from the transmission fluid that went flooding out of our guntruck outside of Azamiya. The front passenger side of our guntruck is metal and wires and suffocating; hot air never stops blowing down on me, and I've nervously tapped against this two-square-foot rubber-coated patch of floor for a few hundred miles. It seems like I almost kick a hole through the armor plated metal when we drive over an IED outside of Nasiriya. Later that night, she cries before taking me off her feet and I understand. Neither of us will ever know why only the primer charge goes off and why molten fragments of copper don't try to rip me off her body.

Part of my right sole is crumbling, melting a little after standing on the metal roof of a building in 130° heat, trying not to slip on empty 5.56 shells that drop hot from above. But I do slip, once, on purpose. I don't tell her so, but I slip, and she falls, face first into a pile of brass. From there, she doesn't have to think about shooting back, and the Special Forces soldiers she is with return fire for her. I see a cousin of mine come sliding in beside me after I slip. Nice move, he says. I nod and push her closer to the sandbags. She pours an entire bottle of water on me when we get back home after this. I want to ask her why she does it, but I can tell she doesn't know either. It just seems like something she ought to do, so I bear it and know that I will dry off next to her pair of tan shower shoes that don't know her the way I know her.

I watch from my spot under the bed as she picks things off the floor and shoves them into her bag. The only things left are some stained t-shirts, a few sets of worn-out uniforms and some gloves.

I'm sorry, she says, but you can't come home with me.

I already knew this, and I know why. I've seen too much here. It doesn't look like it anymore, but I've still got the mud and the smoke and the dust and that soldier's blood in me. I smell of sweat and fear, and my suede tops are stained with tears that only I got to feel. And I know that she can't bring these things back home with her. She sets me in the box with the t-shirts and faded uniforms and takes me to the burn pit. She holds on a little and takes out my laces before throwing me in and pouring diesel on top of the pile. I'm sorry, she says again.

I can say nothing back, and I don't have to because I know she is talking to herself, and to the men she brought over here with her. But she can't say this to them, and they may not understand anyway. Not like I do. So she says it to me. And those words are the last words I hear in Iraq before she pulls the tab on the incendiary grenade and throws almost 4000°F of white phosphorous fire on the pile, and stands in silence in 7.5 wides to watch me return everything I've brought with me back to the dust.

Red Wing Work Boots by Mardi Jaskot

When you meet me, you get the wrong impression. My outside doesn't match my inside. You see and hear a girl, and that's my body and the pitch of my voice, but that's not my soul. Even when I look in the mirror, I still see a stranger there. And so I avoid them, avoid mirrors. I have a girl's body, but my soul is Tommy Lee Jones.

This means I have the soul of a quiet man. His eyes are often hidden under the brim of a hat. When you see his eyes, you might see a mischievous wink or you might see one thousand miles between you and him. The quiet man swallows his pain, turns the spigot off. He feels relief in whiskey and skinny dipping. He is moved by his landscape. He will have lines etched deep across his face, like the dried-up river beds of Texas.

A sundress and sandals belong to another girl. Your daughter, you hope. I am not that girl, so I dress to outfit my soul, not my body. It starts with a baseball cap to shield the eyes, a t-shirt, blue jeans hanging low on the hip, a weathered belt. And the boots. I outfit my soul with black leather Red Wing work boots.

The leather on the rounded steel toe is fuzzy soft and graying, but the rest of the leather is still seal black. The toes are protected by the steel shoe armor, and the double stitching over and around the boot ensures durability. The treads and crevices on the thick black sole are meant for plowing through the mud and gunk. The eight shoelace holes are rimmed in metal to prevent the leather from tearing. The laces are braided and strong, and could serve as a tourniquet. The boot ends above the ankle, offering support for bending, lifting, hunting, hauling. They are heavy, solid and grounding. These work boots are cousins of the tractor.

A girl walks on her toes. A ballerina floats on pointe. A woman stands in stilettos. She defies gravity, but Tommy Lee Jones lets his weight lean back and settle into his heels. You can see it in his slow stride. He walks like steel rods run from his calves, through the heels of his boots, deep into the earth's core. He's moored to the earth. A girl can float, lift off from her toes and into the atmosphere, like a hot air balloon in a skirt. And that might put a sly grin on Tommy Lee's face.

Outfitted in a baseball cap, t-shirt, skinny jeans and my black Red Wing work boots, my mind can forget it's a girl's body. My boots allow my stride to mirror my mind. I feel the mass of me settle into my heels. And anchor me to earth. It's a quiet man's walk. In my boots, my walk is a slow, steady swagger.

Photo permission of Mardi Jaskot.

Sole Sister by Tina Lincer

It wasn't until my sister's 60th birthday last year that I realized how much she loves shoes. I had arrived at her apartment door bearing expensive body lotion and other gifts, but also grocery bags stuffed with discarded clothes. Topping one bag were my old black suede zip-up sneakers.

"Oooh, nice. Anne Klein!" my sister cried, peering at the label. Sitting on the floor, she bent forward and removed her well-worn white sneakers. In a Cinderella moment, she slipped her feet into the AKs, sat up straight and rotated her ankles.

"Are they too big? Do I look ridiculous?" she asked. Though four years older, my sister is the smaller, slighter one of us.

"Walk," said my mother, watching from a chair. She was wearing her own very old shoes, frayed brown leather.

My sister paced the living room into the dining area and back; more of a pivot, actually, in that tiny space. "Think I can get away with these?" she asked.

"They look great," I told her.

"Very snazzy," said my mother.

"I'll keep them," my sister said, cheeks flushed.

Like me, my sister loves shoes. This makes me happy, especially since we've had so little in common. Unlike me, my sister never left home, moved to another city, married or had children. She still lives in the same Queens apartment we grew up in and takes care of our 90-year-old widowed mother.

This AK moment reminds me of a time when cast-offs worked the other way; when the shoe literally was on the other foot. On a sixth grade class trip to the Empire State Building, I wore my sister's ill-fitting, pointy, black patent leather flats, which drew laughs and taunts from the other kids. "Ooh, witch's shoes!"

We were a thrifty family, always in search of a bargain—except, that is, when it came to my mother's 6AA feet. For years, we scoured stores for her perfect shoe fit. Huddled in the back seat of our father's gold Pontiac Catalina, my sister and I were excited, and united, for once; maybe there'd be shoes for us, too. Off we went each Saturday, to Fresh Meadows, Maspeth or Rego Park. We usually ended up at Bonnie's

Bootery in Bayside, because the owner, an Israeli named Eitan, carried the elusive narrow 6s.

These days, there are no shoe stores within easy walking distance of their apartment, and my mother and sister don't drive. I doubt they'd buy, anyway. The old frugality reigns.

What to make of this? Different paths? Maybe. But when I compare their meager, worn shoe collection with my vast one, which includes real Israeli shoes—expensive Naots, made in Tel Aviv—I often feel like—yes—a heel.

Once I arrived at their place with a pair gold of lamé Lacoste sneakers, which I had bummed around in for three summers. They came courtesy of my grown daughter.

"She doesn't want them?" my sister asked.

"She has others," I said.

Truth is, I hated to part with these whimsical hand-me-ups but suspected my sister would adore them. And since she'd started caring for my mother full-time, I wanted to be generous. It was the least I could do. I can never walk away from the fact that, in a strange way, my sister's lack of a more conventional life allows me to step forward in my own life, elsewhere, fairly easily.

And so I continue to stuff bags with random things, eager to bring something new to my sister's world, wanting to ward off the guilt I feel for having left home when she couldn't, or didn't. I shower her with soaps, colorful towels, lipsticks, T-shirts, mugs, calendars, spices, chives from my garden.

And shoes.

Among the items that now enjoy new life on my sister's feet are gray Nike running shoes, black leather flip-flops and pink Polo sneakers with Velcro closures that I purchased for my daughter one year when we were in London. Last summer, when my mother was in a rehab center recovering from a fall, my sister walked six miles to and from the center each day, powered by sheer devotion and those pink Polos.

This winter, my sister lives in brand new waterproof Sorels with tire-tread soles that I picked up at a shoe store closeout.

"Sorels? What's that?" she'd asked when she opened the big box.

"They're Canadian," I said.

She nodded; happy, I think, to learn her footwear's pedigree.

"She couldn't go out without those boots," my mother told me, after the city was hit hard by back-to-back snowstorms.

I picture my sister in her trusty Sorels, sturdy enough to trudge through the Yukon, crossing the busy corner at 73rd and Bell on a bright winter afternoon. In the meantime, I'm thinking about buying her new shoes for her birthday. More boots? Another pair of Nikes? Sheepskin-lined slippers? Or the black Coach sneakers that would be a splurge, but would look so jaunty on her walks to Key Food or CVS?

I could start there, with the grand gesture of Coach shoes. Maybe self-forgiveness would follow.

Photo permission of Tina Lincer.

Crocs by Pamela Laskin

"They are not Crocs!" I say emphatically.

Purple patent leather wedgies, three inches off the ground, adorn my cousin Maggie's feet, exposing flashy, pink toenails.

"They are!" she says, smugly.

"No way!"

"Yes way!"

"They can't be Crocs."

"Why not?" Maggie demands.

"Because Crocs are ugly."

There. I said it. I didn't want to, but I did. Maggie lifts her leg up in the air with the grace of a dancer, so that I may see the lettering, all in caps: CROCS.

"Try them on," she demands.

I am Cinderella with the glass slipper, and the princess of comfort, too. They feel so good on my feet. And they are so passionate: purple passion.

"Do you want me to order you a pair?"

Do I want them? Do I need them? I reflect. Not at all. Must I have them? Surely I must. I dream of the sparkling red-polished toe-nails, and the stares my feet would elicit with these toenails and my purple crocs. I would actually be stylish, even for a day.

"Yes," I shout, "yes; yes," like I am Molly Bloom from *Ulysses* on a mission. Yes I want them. Yes I will wear them. No, I don't need them. All of the above. Maggie proceeds to call the Philadelphia Airport, where they can be directly ordered from the Croc store. It is Sunday. By Tuesday, I am traipsing through the neighborhood wearing my purple crocs and feeling like the Queen of Park Slope, Brooklyn. The shoes remind me of that daring part of me, but also they speak Maggie: exuberant, exciting, daring, free.

Now it is winter, and my feet are drowning in boots. And something else has happened; Maggie is no longer a part of the family's life. She is separating from my cousin; chances are they will be divorced, by next summer, perhaps. As she leaves, as she makes her exit, a change occurs in the wardrobe of my shoes: I am no longer clear on how easy it will be for me to dance around in purple crocs, since the truth of the matter is they are not me, but rather the person I became when Maggie was around: purple, passionate, vibrant. I mostly wear black and gray shoes, and now that the purple part of me is leaving, I am not certain that my affair with the Crocs was anything more than a fling. As Maggie moves on to her new life, my Crocs must soon find their way to the back of my closet, or perhaps on loan to a different person.

Or maybe a different me.

Please, Good People, Remove Your Shoes by Monica Rose

The first time I was asked to remove my shoes at the entrance to someone's living space, I was in college. My friend Ken and I were in Manhattan, visiting his friend Adam. Upon entering Adam's apartment, there were a couple pairs of his shoes against the wall, along with several sets of Chinese slippers. Ken told me, "Leave your shoes here. You can wear a pair of these if you want."

I watched Ken take off his sneakers and slide on some slippers. Without hesitation, I unlaced my Doc Martins and did the same. Adam came down the hallway, bright with sunlight streaming across the walls. There was a noticeable softness in the way Adam moved that made me feel at once warm and comfortable. I wanted to move like that, and somehow, putting on those slippers, the carpet felt more yielding. I was leaving the rest of the world behind by stepping out of one culture and into another. I was leaving behind New York City. What I didn't know was that I was literally leaving behind New York filth by leaving my Docs at the door.

After college, many of my friends moved to Brooklyn. A central hangout became an apartment in a Park Slope brownstone on Saint John's Place. The space became known as 'the women's place' because over the nine years that friends of mine occupied it, no matter who moved out or in, it was always women. As in most New York homes, there was a shoe shelf in the hall at the top of the fourth flight of stairs. And, as if the message around shoe protocol wasn't clear to visitors greeted by a plethora of different sizes and styles of so many shoes and boots that took over the area, a handwritten sign hung on the door: Please, Good People, Remove Your Shoes. With four women, two cats, and a dog, it was hard enough to keep the floors clean without people tracking in dust, dirt, piss and shit from New York City streets and subways. The only exception the women made to this rule was when they hosted parties and one's shoes were integral to the outfit. In New York, fashion often trumps all else, even cleanliness.

When I moved to Ireland, trying to get people to remove their shoes took effort. And, it wasn't a fashion-related resistance; it was just something they didn't care about. But, when I lived alone and operated a kitchen business from my flat, I insisted that visitors take off their shoes. The Galway City Health Board didn't require it for my market stall, but it certainly helped keep my hummus-making business hygienic. Friends understood this reasoning, but when it came to their own living spaces and kitchens (where most socializing happens) it just didn't matter that shoes had stomped around cow-patty and mud-filled fields, or damp dirty pavement.

There were some exceptions to the Irish opposition towards removing footwear. One was at the Galway Zen Dojo, where one *had* to remove one's shoes. There was no sign, but it was obvious. When people walked through the door, the first thing they saw was a place on the floor for leaving shoes, and a rack where kimonos hung. No questions were asked. On the contrary, it was an Asian thing that made complete sense in such a setting as a meditation space. But even with Irish Zen Buddhists, the original culture prevailed. When we rented a bungalow for a five day retreat, no one took off their shoes to go in and out the front door, or to walk around the place, whether it be in the kitchen, halls or bedrooms. When it came time to enter the living room that had been transformed into the meditation room, however, everybody would remove their shoes. After the five days, this became so second nature that when I left and went to visit nearby friends, I walked into their front door and down the hall. When I got to the living room, I bent over to take off my shoes.

Another exception, when I lived in Galway, was my housemate, Niall O'Flynn. Irish as his name, Niall was also a Tai Chi instructor, and so was versed in the Asian ways of shoe etiquette. Between the two of us, we were able to keep a shoe-free house, for the most part. Most of our friends caught on and didn't mind, and for those who chose to leave their shoes on, so be it. The last party we had in that house was twelve years ago, and still comes up in conversations with people who were there. The part that sticks in most heads is what happened when the police showed up. Because it was a moving out party, we invited everybody we knew. I had a decent number of friends and acquaintances, but Niall invited friends from all over the country. People from the many different scenes came: backpackers, drummers, seed savers, Tai Chi and Zen practitioners, Galway market heads, hippies, Irish and English crusties, artists and musicians. We estimated that around one hundred and fifty people came through our house that night. The floor in the front vestibule became covered in several layers of footwear from all walks of life. In order for guests to come in and out, a path had to be cleared, and so shoes were shoved to one side and the other, which resulted in two large mounds of shoes. By the time the noise reached a level that caused the neighbors to call the police, it became a feat to find any matching pairs of shoes, let alone one's own. So, when the party was dispersed, even the two Garda who stood at the door had to shake their heads and laugh and the sight of so many stoned and piss-drunk people searching for their shoes.

A few years ago, when I moved to Park Slope, not far from where the woman's place was, one of the first things I found on Craigslist was a wooden shoe rack for the hall. On it sit my and my roommate's shoes. Above it hangs a yellow and red batik of Buddha's feet that my Irish friend, Roy, brought me back from his trip to India. Most visitors understand the New York thing about shoes, and those who don't are quick to get it. Even my landlord, with whom I'm in a legal battle, will take off his shoes out of respect, before stepping on my living room carpet, and I'm sure he doesn't do so in his own apartment.

Last month, on Christmas Day, I picked up my friend, Antonio, from the rehab center in Manhattan, and drove him home to the Victorian house in Staten Island where several of my closest friends live. Antonio hadn't been home since mid-September because he had suffered a brain hemorrhage, followed by pneumonia, stroke, and a cerebral infection. After two and a half months in ICU, during which time we didn't know if he'd live or die, Antonio woke up. He spent another month in rehab, learning how to sit up, walk, talk, swallow, eat, and take care of himself all over again. We had to find him comfortable shoes that were easy to slip off and on, but he still needed a shoe-horn as long as a yard-stick in order to get his heel down all the way. His progress was going so well that the doctors agreed to a day pass so that Antonio could go home for Christmas. I picked him up early in the morning, and wheeled him outside the rehab center's doors on Madison Avenue. When the cold air greeted him—his first taste of fresh air in an entire season—his eyes filled with tears.

"I feel like I just got out of jail," he said, crying, as we drove down FDR Drive.

Once at the house, it took some time to get the walker and help ease a dazed Antonio out of the car. Step by slow step, we walked to the front of the house, switched the walker off with the cane, and went carefully up the three front stairs. In the entryway, I didn't bother removing my boots. I was intent on getting him over the last step of the threshold, where Alice and Marigold, ages three and five, were waiting with smiles. I was especially moved to see Marigold ready to hug Antonio, because she had withdrawn that time we took her to ICU, and didn't want to visit him in rehab. We were all concerned that she would take a while to warm back up to him. But there she stood, unreserved in her excitement to have him home. I motioned Antonio's arm, toward the step, but he wasn't looking at the waiting girls. He was leaning his fragile body over so that he could remove his shoes. Unbalanced as he was, Antonio was able to complete this task, and only then did he straighten up, step into the house and embrace the children he had missed so much. This stunning act of normalcy moved me to tears, and I am still astounded by how meaningful such a simple ritual can be.

Laskin, Di Iorio, Clark

III. CODA:
THOUGHTS FOR
THE FUTURE

Shoes by Phebus Etienne

1966-2007
Later, I remembered shoes.

"Shoes?" my aunt questioned
as I rummaged through my mother's closet.
We had chosen a coffin with silver etchings,
then moved along the rack of chiffon dresses,
some garnished with pearls at the neckline
and cuff. I thought of the wedding
my mother hadn't lived to see
before buying a tea-length dress
in cornflower blue. The rosary
I brought to her from Rome
would fall gracefully on the lace
gloves covering the incisions
made by the intravenous lines. As I examined

patent leather pumps, my aunt insisted,
"Haitians do not put shoes on the dead."
It makes it easier for wandering spirits
to step over the offerings, the candles,
dried thorns and retrace their steps
to find the living. I buy
silk slippers with a satin bow,
spray the white undergarments
with my mother's favorite perfume.
Each time I visit her grave, I clear
sharp rocks on the path leading home.
Sometimes I crumble
pieces of the rum cake she enjoyed along the road,
sit under the calabash and wait to be found.

Forward by Pamela Laskin

February 10, 2010: "Later I remember the shoes." The words of this brilliant young Haitian poet, now deceased, bring to my mind not only her own shoes, and those she thought of buying for her mother's funeral, but the multitude of shoes being gathered for the victims of the earthquake in Haiti. Crunch Gym in New York City is doing a shoe drive, so I collect my excess shoes to bring over: my gift, my offering. I know that in the months ahead, thousands of young children will attend funerals—or maybe not—since many people who have died in the earthquake of January 12th cannot be found amidst the debris. As of February 2010, seventy thousand bodies have been buried in mass graves, while assorted body parts have been extracted from the rubble: unidentified arms and torsos and legs. This earthquake—a 7.0 on the Richter scale—wreaked havoc and destruction on a country already steeped in poverty and disaster. Now 23,000 have officially been declared dead in Port-au-Prince, 25,000 residences have been destroyed, and at least 30,000 commercial buildings have collapsed. Men, women and children who previously walked around in bare feet now must contend with the broken glass and chipped plaster that line the streets like tombstones. And there are too many orphaned children, unmoored in a sea of destruction.

As I gather the shoes in my family's closet: my husband's; my daughter's; my son's; but mostly mine, I feel an odd mixture of gratitude and guilt. How fortunate I am, to live in a society where I can afford this indulgence. Yet, as I pack up this abundance to send to Haiti, it reminds me of how trapped I am in the culture of consumerism. How could I possibly own twenty pairs of different colored, unused foot attire, when in other parts of the world, just one pair is a luxury? Yet again, I face the monster of injustice: this is a world where you don't have to step beyond a cultural border to observe the traumatic hierarchy of the haves and have-nots. Shoes—*my* shoes—are a symbol; I am clearly "the other."

So, for better or for worse, I dress my feet in quaint pleasures daily, and am often reminded this is overly whimsical. This sometimes becomes a source of anxiety when there is a natural disaster, now an earthquake, which has left millions homeless. Being shoeless may be among the least of their problems, but certainly I need not be so frivolous and purchase yet another pair of shoes, when the rest of the world is mourning their losses.

At the end of this book, I discuss the possibility of a shoeless universe in which the hierarchy of status and class would be diminished. Phebus Etienne, the author of the magnificent poem "Shoes," chooses black patent leather pumps to put on her dead mother's feet, but her aunt tells her that, "Haitians do not put shoes on the dead." It makes it easier "for the wandering spirits to step over the offerings, the candles, dried thorns and retrace their steps to find the living." The fantasy of bare feet articulates the need to directly experience the world's offerings, be it the frigid cold or the torturous heat, and also to be able to navigate the bridge between the living and the dead. It is impossible to imagine ascending heaven's stairs or descending into Hades' bowels with our feet strapped into a pair of Manolo Blahnik heels. More significant is the challenge of purchasing such an extravagant item, or even several less expensive pairs, in this climate of chronic tragedy; but still, I cannot commit to staying out of a shoe store—yet!

Later I remember shoes. The fantasy is still vibrant, but the bloodstream of tragedy and recession will keep it tempered.

Bunions by Mary Frankel

Mark Twain says, "Clothes make the man."[1] I say, "Shoes make the woman." And I am that woman…I like to show my inside on my outside. Inside, I am an artist—a lover of language, literature, art, ideas and beauty. However after years of after-school art classes and more as an adult, I realized that art was more than the sum of mastering the craft and technique. As one of my photography teachers told me, "Now you know everything there is to know about *how* to do it. Now you have to find your voice." What do I want to say, to observe, to comment upon in the world through my camera? What can I contribute that is new, sage, even wry? After I earned my master's degree and I considered getting a doctorate, I thought the same thoughts: What could I contribute to the literature that would be unique and enlightening? More important to both questions, what would engage me over the years to make the struggle worthwhile? After much thought, the answer was *shoes*.

I became aware of shoes when I graduated from college and ventured out into the big pond, aka the real world, where I discovered that smarts and style made a difference. In the mid 60s and 70s, women had the opportunity to be in the larger workforce, in that meaningful jobs were now open to us. Prior to that time, the Help Wanted pages of the newspaper were divided into "Men" and "Women" sections and all the jobs under "Women" were secretary, nurse or assistant to some man. I was on the cusp of the "revolution" in employment. I was educated, a quick study, AND had a unique style. Part of the package was my petite-ness and my attention to the details of my outside presentation. I learned to put myself together, including sweet shoes. Having developed bunions in my 20s (according to my mother because I wore high heels—but what about heredity, Mom?—because you have them, too) I took it as my duty as a professional to buy only the best, comfortable yet attractive shoes. Then I discovered Nordstrom—a fantasyland come true for my Cinderella size 5 feet—on a business trip to California. My shoe "claim to fame" is buying nine pairs of shoes in one fateful afternoon, having them shipped back to the East Coast, and last but not least, having someone from Nordstrom offer to drive me back to my hotel. That is what I call a strike.

---

1   Mark Twain's full quote is as follows: "Clothes make the man. Naked people have little or no influence on society."

Now I am retired from the professional life I never dared envision for myself; assistant and associate deanships at major universities and medical schools. I no longer need to "dress for success." Nonetheless, my love of shoes remains intact and in practice. Now the bunions are no longer an excuse for buying the best shoes; they are more a reminder of my aging, changing self. And as I learn to accept my limitations (no more high heels) and search for the most comfortable, bunion-hiding, stylish yet age appropriate shoes, my lust endures. Wasn't it Elizabeth Kubler-Ross who posited that acceptance is the last stage before death? Well, not for me. I'm still workin' the shoes.

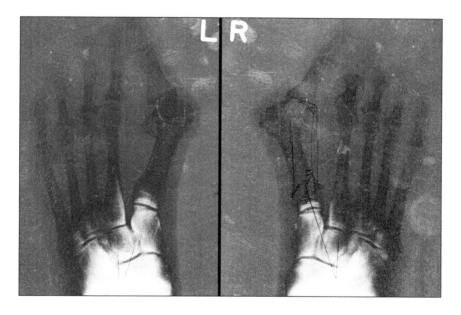

Photo permission of Mary Frankel.

Stilettos and Power: What I Did for...
Love? Money? Power? by Johanna Youner, DPM, FACFAS

From women of a certain age (that is, over forty) I hear the refrain every day. "I have a closet full of beautiful shoes, and none of them are comfortable! Can you operate on me to make me fit into my shoes?"

The variations on this theme are (from women in their thirties), "My closet looks like Carrie Bradshaw's," meaning "filled with fanciful, sexy high heels." Over forty, the refrain goes something like, "My closet looks like Imelda Marcos' closet," meaning, "My poor closet contains 800 pairs of unworn shoes." With a pair of Manolo Blahnik stilettos retailing for over five hundred dollars, the investment is significant, especially if we are unable to wear these shoes

Why do we torture ourselves?

Women have a history of self-scarification in the name of cultural significance. The ritual of foot binding to create a pair of sexy, but useless, feet went on in China until the white Christian missionaries got hold of the Chinese women in the early 20th century. The binding ritual denoted higher status in society. Foot binding meant you were a sexualized object, not a worker in the fields. A woman with bound feet was unable to walk without assistance. The bound foot itself was also a sexualized object, as the bound foot was used during sex as an adjunct vagina.

The foot binding process started at age 6, with nightly binding with long linen cloths. The binding was done every evening by a female relative. The lesser toes were bound under the front of the foot, and the whole foot was bound together, trying to meet the heel to the toe area. Only the great toe was left alone.

The pain of literally breaking growing bones was only part of the ritual. The risks of foot binding included infection and gangrene. In about two years, the binding was completed and the bound foot was, at most, four inches long, with the curve under the foot being the sexualized area.

In modern times, we look at this ritual and consider it barbaric. How much more barbaric is it to shove one's foot into a shoe that looks nothing like the purpose to which it was born, i.e., to protect the foot and control walking?

My most basic shoe advice to women who cannot find a comfortable shoe to wear is simple. Compare your foot to the shoe you are considering. If the shoe does not resemble a foot, chances are, this is not a comfortable shoe.

Fashion dictates the height of shoes. The addition of a platform under the forefoot can make a formerly 4" stiletto into a 6" heel. This platform is modern and sexy. The height of the heel adds slimness to the body, a curve to the back, bum, breasts and calves. One looks sexier and thinner with the addition of the heel. But with the cost of long-term high heels being deformities such as painful bunions, hammer toes, and neuromas, as well as the more mundane corns and calluses, we can ask, "At what price for beauty?"

Lawyers say that jurors in uncomfortable shoes are not easily swayed. As a Park Avenue podiatric surgeon with twenty years of experience, I have found a similar ethic in women and their high heels. High-end saleswomen in diverse fields are very unwilling to part with their high heels. These women find power in their heels. Their self-worth in business comes partly through their uniforms of heels and suits. These businesswomen use their heels and outfits as suits of armor in a difficult world. Despite my common-sense approach to their corns, calluses and foot pain, stiletto-wearing businesswomen who see these heels as part of their uniform are simply unwilling to part with their heels, no matter what the physical price. Looking at their shoes, the three-inch heels and pointed toes appear as weapons in the male-dominated world of business. Their gym-toned bodies and tight business suits usually indicate that these women, despite looking for a cure for their pain, are not going to negotiate their heels to a lower spike, or thicker heel. Many women are willing to undergo painful surgeries to shorten their toes, simply to fit into their shoes.

The human body is extremely adaptable, and will mold itself to the job at hand. If you place an average, square-shaped foot into a stiletto shoe, the foot will become contracted. The back of the leg will also contract, forcing the Achilles tendon to become shorter. Recent studies have shown that the muscle cells in the Achilles tendon are changed and shortened after two years of wearing high heels. One of the first signs of the economic downturn in 2008 in New York City was real estate brokers pounding the pavement in their high heels to sell property in a time of panic. These brokers developed stress fractures, and ended up wearing huge cam walkers (healing, ski-boot type affairs) for six weeks, instead of their former fabulous shoes.

The use of injectable fillers has helped this arena of pain and hammertoes. A difficult and painful hammer toe can temporarily be helped with fillers like Juvederm. The process of this simple, albeit expensive, treatment can help a woman fit into her shoes more comfortably, but there are laws of nature at work here. If you continue to put your foot into ill-fitting shoes, a situation will be created by the deforming forces of the shoe. These deforming forces will create a deformed foot, which is anathema to the sexy, capable female ideal we are trying to project. A comfortable solution of wearing a more comfortable shoe day-to-day, and changing into the shoes we need for our competitive, challenging situations is the obvious answer.

I absolutely respect a woman's desire to look beautiful and sexy for her date, for an event, or to appear powerful at a business meeting. Walking around New York City in high heels, although glamorous, is a high price to pay for beauty. Have we not, as women, come further than purposely deforming our feet for the sake of beauty and power?

Carla Bruni-Sarkozy wears ballet flats. As the wife of the President of the French Republic, Nicolas Sarkozy, she plays on the world's stage. Academy Award-winning director Sofia Coppola is known for her gentle but spot-on fashion sense. In the powerful arena of film making, she wears flats as her calling card. These women are not grasping for an identity or hiding behind antiquated and time-honored shoe gear to indicate their ability and power. Their works speak for themselves.

So why do we do this to ourselves? The costs of wearing improper shoes are so high. Do we really want a permanent reminder, via neuromas and other painful foot scars, of the battles of yesteryear, waged in our stilettos? My advice is simple: Wear what is comfortable. Wear what fits. A two-inch heel should be enough power to close the deal. A client is not wagering a multi-million dollar deal on the strength of your shoes. However beautiful, works of art, including unwearable shoes, should be relegated to fashion museums, not to our feet. Be kind to your body. It will thank you.

Those Look Comfortable by Rebecca Minnich

I am not someone to whom anyone is ever going to say, "Wow! Those shoes look great!" It's all right. I have made peace with this. What I hear instead are words as dreaded as they are predictable: "Those look comfortable." Let's face it. "Those look comfortable" is polite phrasing for "Where did you get them so I can tell my 89-year-old Aunt Mildred?"

I noticed a friend's pair of Clark loafers that I felt had a sturdy, yet sleek look. I wondered if I could fit into them. To my compliments she replied, "Thanks. I think they're a good compromise. They don't cause me pain, yet they don't quite say, 'I have entirely given up.'"

My shoes, for the record, *do* say, "I have entirely given up." In fact, they have gone beyond giving up, and are now beseeching me to put them out of their misery and let them slink away with the remainder of their dignity intact, perhaps into a Salvation Army bin. But the thing about healthy shoes is that they really *do* last for years, and if you're going to spend a hundred bucks, they should, damn it.

The story of how I ended up with a closet full of practical, ergonomic footwear that excludes high heels, flip-flops, thongs between any toes, pumps, platforms, or anything that could remotely be construed as sexy is a two-part tale: 1. Four-inch-wide feet, (a cruel joke of heredity) and 2. Bunions (see point one).

Some background is probably in order. Most women's shoes, as all females know but rarely want to admit, are not designed for actual feet. They are meant to decorate the delightfully slender and tiny lower appendages of elves, fairies, and wood sprites. Tricked out with ankle-slicing straps, tendonitis-inducing pointy toes, shiny buckles that don't actually buckle anything, soled with either a slip of rubber the thickness of a communion wafer or vertiginous elevated heels that ring out like gunshots and crack one's molars with each footfall, these shoes are not actually meant to carry the weight of a human being.

I can already hear female voices rising in protest: "But I can find shoes that are both comfortable *and* fashionable! Look! See?" And I have looked, and I do see. Very cute. And I'm happy for you. Really, I am. But there are three problems with this defense. The first, oh, ye of the cute-yet-fashionable shoes, is that chances are, your size seven-to-nine feet measure less than four inches across.

Go ahead, measure them. I'll wait.

The width of mine, believe it or not, prevents me from even considering slipping my size eight-and-a-half foot into eighty-five percent of women's shoes. I can tell just by looking at them whether it's worth it to try them on or just cut to the chase and make my way to the wide-width, problem-feet, limping-old-lady section of the shoe store to find the shoes I can actually wear.

The second problem is this: Just how many stores did you go to, how many hours did you spend looking, how many pairs did you try on, and how much did you shell out for those shoes that are both comfortable and fashionable? In other words, is this acquisition of the fashionable-yet-comfortable woman's shoe something that a person living with actual financial and time constraints can undertake? Or must one adopt a *Sex and the City* lifestyle of shopping four hours a day, interspersed by gossip at the Russian Tea Room, aerobics at Crunch, and eating small food with gal pals in Soho bistros?

The third problem is the most intractable, and here I refer to the painful, bony protuberance of the first metatarsal known as the bunion. Do you have them, I ask? If not, we're done here. To hell with your damn shoes.

My favorite question, on the odd occasions when I mention bunions in mixed company, is usually asked by men: "Now how is it different from a corn? Can you, like, shave it off with a pumice stone?"

Oh, innocence. Oh, blissful ignorance.

The bunion is caused by the normal spread of the five human toes being constricted and crushed together into shoes that push the toes together into an unnatural point. In other words, women's shoes. This is why ninety percent of bunion sufferers are women. (The rest are drag queens or men with a penchant for tight cowboy boots.) The constriction deforms the big toe bone, or first metatarsal from its straight, weight-bearing status to being buckled and folded inward at the second joint, the place where it joins to the ball of the foot. Over time, the angle of the bend gets more acute, until the big toe folds over the second toe, leaving a grotesque, pointy, bony growth jutting out from the inside edge of the foot, causing agonizing, shooting pains up the arch of the foot and all the way up the shins of the leg. It also plays havoc with balance and, as it grows over time, eventually makes running and dancing impossible.

Bunion surgery is often recommended at this point. This usually involves breaking the bone, resetting it, and removing several grams of lumpy bone matter from the joint so it can function normally again. In minor cases, laser surgery can be performed, but it isn't as effective. Bunion surgery can cost several thousand dollars and it is common for insurance companies to reject the claims, unless a person is basically crippled from the condition.

But those pumps. They're just so cute, aren't they? And men love them. Right?

Throughout my adult life, I have been waiting for women to rise up in rebellion against shoes that destroy our feet. It hasn't happened yet, and perhaps won't. The obsession with sexy footwear is too dear to the female ego. What has happened in lieu of revolution, and I find this interesting, is a quiet subversion in the form of anti-fashion trends. A couple of summers ago, the screw-you flag took the form of monstrosities called Crocs, sandal-clogs so wide as to be very nearly circular, dotted with giant Swiss-cheese holes, big enough to air out the hugest of bunions and dry the sweat that inevitably accumulates within shoes made entirely of petroleum by-products. Available in various shades of crap brown, bland pastels and primary colors, they pick up dirt as easily as chewed gum and look about as attractive. In the summer of 2008, the subway floors were lurid with them in all sizes, and the streets echoed with their stumping, shuffling footfalls. The trend has started to die out a bit, but is still strong among children and people in the Midwest.

Over the past two winters, legions of young women, and some not so young, have fallen under the spell of Uggs; fat, squishy, suede moon boots with no heel, no sole structure, tube-like ankles and a bedroom-slipper fuzzy lining. They're so shapeless that there seems to be no difference between the right one and the left one. Just grab whichever; it doesn't matter. This is a look that says "Who the fuck cares?" Or perhaps it says, "I have a pair of Manolo Blahniks in my closet, but my feet hurt so goddamn much that this is what I'm wearing? Okay? You got a problem with that?"

I have promised myself I will not stoop to these trends. This is a matter of personal integrity. Until the female footwear revolution is well underway, I will continue to try not to cringe when I see women in their seventies wearing the exact same pair of Merrell walking shoes as mine. I'll try to tell myself my Birkenstocks are an investment in healthy aging, in life without a limp. That there is more to life than the illusive image of the sexy foot. That I will catch that cab before the chick in the stilettos.

And I won't even feel bad about it.

New Balance by Mary Morris

I'm no Cinderella. I've never been the kind of girl to let a glass slipper determine my fate. Despite my mother and her fashion sense, I've always lived more in my head. I've been ambivalent, to say the least. As a young woman, I liked to wear shoes, but I hated to buy them. This is a deep-tissue response. Like any woman, I own my share of shoes—the usual heels and sling backs, flip-flops and cowgirl boots, short boots, tall boots. Mephisto sandals, and, tucked somewhere in my closet, there's an old pair of Maud Frizons. It's true that, in my youth, shoes let me grow taller, sexier. But it was a troubled connection, at best.

Ah, women and their shoes. To the chagrin of my mother (whom I don't think I've ever seen out of a pair of patent pumps) I'm a far cry from Elle Woods, the character Reese Witherspoon played in "Legally Blonde." There's a wonderful moment when Elle realizes a prosecution witness could not have been having an affair with the woman accused of murdering her husband, because this particular witness is gay. And she realizes it because, as she taps her foot at a drinking fountain, the witness spews, "Don't tap your last season's Prada at me." Elle has a *eureka!* moment. Only a gay man would know that she's wearing last season's Prada; hence, he is lying on the stand.

Cinderella, "Legally Blonde"—fates are made and broken with a pair of shoes. But alas, not for me. Yes, I'll wear shoes. If I must, I'll even buy them. I blame this ambivalence, as I blame most things of this ilk, on my mother. Shoes were a huge part of my mother's life. Well, clothes in general were. My mother once studied fashion design at the Art Institute of Chicago. Her life was built around accessories—as if she'd stepped right out of Coco Chanel's playbook. Basic black, or beige. Lots of purses, scarves, jewelry—and, of course, shoes.

In my youth, my shoes were always purchased at Fell's Shoes. Debbie Fell was, and still is, one of my closest friends, and the Fell family pretty much cornered the market on fashion in my small suburban town. Still, I hated being dragged there—but it was unavoidable.

A few times a year, my mother and I would make our pilgrimage to Fell's, where my foot was measured with that X-ray thing they used to do—dare I say it?—fifty years ago. Even now, I can see the skeletal outline of my feet. Like a costume I'd wear for Halloween. And then the shoes would come out, and my mother would make her selection. The saddle shoes, the black patent pumps, the gym shoes, those winter boots that old ladies might wear.

So I never really felt that connected to my feet, or to the shoes I put on. Shoes were just something I had to do, like walking the dog and getting an oil check on my car—until the time came, just a few years ago, when I couldn't wear them. I couldn't even walk a step.

❧

On a February morning in 2008, I turned to my husband Larry and said, "Let's go skating." Ice skating is something I've done all my life, and I used to do it very well. This was on the first day of a much-anticipated six month sabbatical. But an hour into it, I fell on the ice, twisting my ankle. When offered an ambulance, I refused. I had places to go—Morocco and Spain—and many plans for the next several months.

Instead, I went home. An hour later, I realized I needed to get to the hospital. On the way, I lost my balance, tumbled down my front steps and watched as my foot went in directions I didn't know were physically possible.

And apparently, they are not.

I shattered my fibula. It was a catastrophic injury, and I found myself housebound, spending my days canceling all the plans I'd made. I was also "non-weight bearing," words I have come to dread. I couldn't go outside. I couldn't even go up and down my stairs. And, beyond this, I was incredibly depressed.

A few weeks after my fall, I went on my first big outing—to see my surgeon, who was going to remove my "soft" cast and put on a hard one. I have a good rapport with him. He is a handsome, affable, youngish man, with a good handshake, as Larry was quick to point out. But when he unwrapped my foot to remove the stitches, I wanted to clobber him with my crutch.

This was the first time I saw the monster foot. One that must have gotten caught in a bear trap. Clearly not a part of my body. Still, I tried to put on a good face. "We're going to put on your hard cast now," he told me, smiling as I smiled back, wondering if the appendage at the end of my leg would ever look like my own. "I have two colors. I guess you'd call these mustard and orange." And he held up what looked like bicycle reflector tape.

It was then that something deep—some visceral instinct took over. I stared, dumbfounded, at my surgeon, trained at the Hospital for Special Surgery, whose hourly rate is probably close to my monthly salary. "Doctor," I said. "I can't do mustard or orange."

"I don't understand."

Behind him his nurse froze. The technical assistant stopped moving. I don't think they'd ever heard anyone defy him. He stared at me, bewildered.

"Do I look like the kind of girl who wears neon?"

He still didn't get it.

"I need a neutral color," I sighed.

"A neutral color? What's that?"

"You know, beige, brown, gray. Something I can wear with anything."

He pulled himself up and turned to his nurse. "She needs a neutral color." The nurse was about to shrug, when he turned to her and said, "See what you can find."

There was a flurry of activity, and then they all returned with their hands full of navy and charcoal and black bandage tape. I inspected the trove. "Charcoal," I declared. So for the next four weeks I lived with my charcoal cast. I was, in fact, rather proud of it. I wouldn't let anyone sign it (though I can't say anyone really wanted to). I just liked the look of it.

This isn't easy to admit, but—my cast had style.

But then it was time for it to be removed, and it was, and I was told to go home and walk. And I couldn't. I couldn't cross the street. I couldn't walk to the corner for a quart of milk. A week later, I was back in my surgeon's office. "When will I be normal again?" I asked, tears sliding down my face. He had betrayed me.

"Normal. What do you mean?"

I explained to him that, in this instance, normal meant "the way I was before." Long walks in the park, strolling the city, racing down subway stairs. He shook his head. "I'm happy you're walking at all," he told me. "I wasn't sure you would."

A race horse, he told me, is put down for less.

❦

Do you know that, after an accident like this, your foot doesn't remember its relationship to the ground? It doesn't know how to balance or stand upright. So I had to start from scratch. Since this accident, the two surgeries it required, and months of rehab, I've come to value my feet, and the shoes I put on them. I pay homage to that distant part of my body which I never gave a hoot about before.

Despite the fact that it is actually better for me to walk in heels, I worry about falling. I've become one of those women who walks the city in New Balance and keeps a pair of sandals or low heels in my bag. When I see girls parading around in those four inch stiletto heels, I'm like one of those crazy old women who wants to go up and warn them. And I always strap my sandals on, even if I'm just going to the store.

I've come to look at shoes. Will they be comfortable? Will they support my feet? And, yes, are they in style? If not, they go on the street. I have in some ways become my mother's daughter, something I'd resisted for so long.

Shortly before she died, my mother was in the hospital for a broken hip. I was with her when she learned that she was going home that day. "Show me my clothes," she ordered me. "I want to see what I'll be going home in."

"Mom, I said, "they're the same clothes you arrived in."

"I want to see them," she insisted.

So I showed her the beige slacks and white silk blouse, the beige jacket, her underwear and hose, the coat she'd wear—one at a time. She frowned, pursing her lips. "Is that all?"

"Yes, that's it, Mom. It's all here."

A few hours later her caregiver arrived, and she made the same request. "But, Mom," I told her, "I just showed you everything."

"No!" my 99 year old mother, who could not recall if I am married or if I have one child or two, exclaimed, "You didn't show me my shoes."

Our Soles by Emma Dora Ruth Ziegellaub Eichler

Black Sauconys are Bobby's only pair of shoes.
Silver squiggles like whiskers framing white laces
and white rubber sidewalls sandwiched by black sole
glow on a nighttime bowling alley. In synthetic siding,
bike pedals rip holes,
gone the next day, his sneakers somehow clean again. The heels
never wear down; he never outgrew walking on tip-toes.

Black suede so worn and hardened on the toes,
it has gone from shiny back to soft again. Lee owns shoes—
furry brown mocs—but is unconcerned by peeling heels;
all he wears are these black Adidas, with dog-chewed laces
and frayed ends impossible to rethread through holes.
They have yet to come undone; he refuses to replace his rubber soul.

For school, Emily insists on footwear with a thick soul:
mesh black athletic sneakers, combat boots with reinforced toes,
knocking against bare feet—socks will just develop holes.
She got Annie to take her shopping but wouldn't try other shoes,
though Annie got her to buy skinny jeans; she likes tightening laces,
unlike the boys who won't bother. For dances, she wears heels.

Kelly wears Uggs, flats, and Keds; she boycotts only heels
for the fraying green threads and rusted rivets of her oldest Converse.
Her soul
is hard to make out among purple cameo, wild cat prints,
knotted laces
of basketball sneaks swung over shoulder, toes
bouncing on back. We own two pairs of identical shoes—
each copied one from the other; with them, we patch holes.

The theory that sex can be predicted by footwear has holes;
it determines that, though he doesn't wear heels,
Marley's not male because it's hard to keep track of all his shoes,
less varied than those of a girl; he has a more decided sole.
Pairs red, blue, white, and black have rubber deflector toes,
flap around his skinny ankles with ground-dragging laces.

Valeriya owns more shoes than days in a month but no laces.
(Did she never learn how to tie them?) She has peep-holes
and closed fronts forming a smooth scale from peaked to pointed toes.
Shiny cream patent and silver reptile leather, they all share the heels,
save the denim-stained Pumas with pink side stripes and
grooved soles.
She tells me that what sets us apart are our shoes.

I wear round fronts, never her pointy toes or peep-holes.
What laces our souls together are our shoes:
I wear flats and she wears heels.

Ethical Dilemma by Elana Bell

Another unexpected rainstorm in New York, and I am caught unprepared, leaving work in a pair of soft leather oxfords, now soaked through to the socks. My toes are icy, but because this is New York City, I can't go home—a friend is performing in less than an hour, and there is no way I can make it to Brooklyn and back in time for her show. Plus, I don't totally mind the fact that I have to buy myself a pair of stylish, water-resistant shoes. No one can accuse me of frivolity in this case, right? My feet are completely soaked, for God's sake!

I duck into SHOE MANIA at Union Square, a shoe shopper's paradise. The walls are lined with everything from *New Balance* to *Cole Haan*, and a driving techno beat pulsing through the stereo seems, I could almost swear, to have the subliminal message "buy, buy, buy." But this evening I am here with a purpose, and I do not veer from my course. "Waterproof boots, size nine," I say, when one of the many the salesmen asks if he can help me. "Not plastic. I want something warm." He returns with two pairs. One pair is beige, lined with sheep shearling. I try them on, but the color doesn't do anything for me. The other pair is black suede, with rabbit fur.

"These are waterproof?" I ask, somewhat suspiciously.

He points to the clearly-labeled tag. WATERPROOF, it says.

"Anyway, I don't wear animal fur."

He shrugs. "Try them on." I slip the boots over my jeans, and my feet are suddenly clouded in warmth. I feel like I have wrapped my feet in shoe-manna, in my baby blanket—no, in a womb. My feet are now in their own womb. They will never be cold again. I walk to the mirror. The boots look incredible—sexy in that chic, clunky way. I look outside at the rain, which shows no signs of shifting.

"So?" he asks, smiling.

"I don't like to buy products made of animal fur," I say, trying to keep the conviction in my tone.

"But you wear leather, don't you?"

"That's different," I say sharply, although I can't seem to remember exactly *how* at this moment.

"Look, either way, the rabbit is already dead. He doesn't care."

"And you are a very good salesman," I say, smiling. "You make a good point, but I still don't feel right about it."

"Listen, I don't want you to buy the boots if you are going to feel bad. Really. But think about it. Nothing you do can change the fate for this rabbit. He was meant to die, to be made into boots. This was God's will, not yours or mine."

I definitely was not expecting the conversation to have taken this turn. I stand up, so we are eye to eye, my feet still snug in the delicious warmth of the boots. "That may be true, but if I buy these boots, then I am contributing to more rabbits being killed for their fur."

"You are such a good woman," he says, in his honeyed voice.

"Too good." I snort.

"Listen. I am a Muslim man, from Egypt."

I nod, unsure of where this is going.

"So, you know we are commanded to eat only halal meat, right?"

I nod again.

"Well," he continues, "when I first came to this country I only ate halal meat. And I am not talking about going to a little stand with shish kabab and some rice. I mean, I would go all the way to the end of Brooklyn to pick my goat or cow, and the butcher would slaughter it right there."

"Wow," I say, looking at my watch.

"Here's my point. After a few months, I stopped doing that. Too much work, you know. And now, I eat regular meat like everybody else. Sometimes," his voice lowers to a whisper, "I even eat pork."

I walk back and forth through the narrow aisles of the store. I call my boyfriend to get some outside reassurance, to hear him tell me that I am not a bad person if I buy these boots, but there is no answer. I call my best friend. No answer. I walk back to the mirror and take one more look at the dead rabbits on my feet. I head to the register and pull out my credit card. "I'll be wearing these out," I say, and walk confidently into the rain, coming down harder than before.

Tom's by Pamela Laskin

I can't buy new shoes; there is a recession. It is 2009, and since our bright, young, African-American star—Obama—has been elected to office, things have not gotten better. Daily, more people are losing their jobs. The Christmas bells ring out a discordant note this holiday season. Forget about buying those brand new, beautiful, black riding boots, whose leather is as soft as an infant's skin. They cost three hundred dollars. If I had three hundred dollars to burn, I would donate it to a charity.

This season shall be a shoeless one, or I can rely on the dozens of boots, the decades of furnished flats that barely fit in my closet. Perhaps I will purchase a pair of Toms sneakers. Toms are the only shoes I feel justified in buying this year.

Tom (that is his name) came up with a brilliant idea: by simply purchasing a pair of Toms shoes, you can, for example, have a direct impact on the life of someone in Ethiopia. There is a debilitating disease, potoconiosis, that plagues those who walk barefoot in silica-rich soil. Podo is 100% preventable, simply by wearing shoes, a luxury many people in this part of the world can not afford.

If I purchase a pair of Toms sneakers, someone, somewhere, who has, up until this time, been shoeless, will now own a pair of shoes. This is the pay-it-forward concept: give to someone, which will propel more giving—the snowball effect of generosity.

I have always thought of myself as a generous person, but the truth of the matter is, if I had fifty dollars to purchase black velvet ballet flats or give to someone in need, I would probably choose the flats.

Until now. Now I will treat myself to the forest green Toms flats, in which, my daughter insists, you can walk for miles. I will walk many miles on the hard New York City pavement, and feel fortunate that God gave me the power to walk, and the ability to go into Eric's high-end shoe store and buy a pricy pair—on occasion.

For now I am a Toms gal, and would feel guilty to be otherwise, as another round of lay-offs ushers in the New Year. And this will be a good year, hopefully, 2010, a great year for the countless unemployed, and a good year for me, too, with my brand new Toms shoes, ones which dress the feet of another young woman halfway across the world, a person who never thought she would ever have shoes on her feet.

Winter Dream No. 24 (These Boots Are Made)
by Laura Hinton

i was in the shoe store and was buying shoes in the dream but then in
the dream i was attracted to boots i needed them *chic and warm* long
fur all around the edges angora or a wild cat not just edges but about
a third of the boot was long and hairy *chic and warm* i needed them
those booties so i asked the price i was always looking for sales in life
like in the dream i love sales the boots on sale they made me feel
chic and warm in the dream looking at the boots i realized something
strong something wrong strong that i was a shopping addict

one that
tried to resist the boots in the dream but found i couldn't the addict
one was too strong so i dreamed i was Lucille Ball and hid the fact i
was buying the boots from my husband in fact
they were such a great deal marked down all the way from
$$436
chic and warm
dollars all the way down to
$$150
chic and warm
dollars but because it was no longer summer but
chic and warm
winter the boots were marked back up to now
$$300
chic and warm
dollars so
chic and warm
i said and what a deal i am attracted to the feel of the boots i need
them
chic and warm angora or wild cat so i won't tell my husband the fact
and i didn't
tell him

the only part i didn't like in the dream about the boots was the sole reversal the side of the sole containing not a little dial not a phone like the detective from Get Smart in the '60's but a big dial that went round and round and the dial had no purpose i did not know why the boots *chic and warm*
had a dial

And thus the dream ended on a lie

My husband said this is not a liar's dream but a dream about walking away

Artwork permission of Elizabeth New.

The Future by Pamela Laskin

I dream a shoeless universe. Everyone—in every part of the world—prances around in bare feet, not just on hard city-cement streets, but on pebbled dirt roads; on warm-sandy beaches; on ranches rampant with the smell of manure. In my mind's Utopia, it is a Green planet, and we can walk it barefoot.

Walking without a wardrobe means taking in every terrific and terrifying sensation: the horrible heat of an Arizona summer or the treacherous tundra of the Alaskan wilderness. It is possible to burn your bunions or freeze your toes, since shoes are obsolete. Snowstorms piled six feet high with ice and powdered flakes demand an ability to persevere, combined with a desire to rise to the challenge. People who have survived wars have spoken of treks through the brambles and branches of forests with nothing on their feet. The point is, there are survivors, ones who may have spent years without creature comforts. We have grown too comfortable, and this desire propels us not to simply take care of basic needs, but to aspire toward new levels of excess. People need, at the most, perhaps three pairs of shoes, but as Imelda Marcos, wife of the former president of the Philippines has demonstrated, a woman can fill her closet with hundreds of pairs of sneakers, clogs, sandals, heels, but still it is not enough. This is a culture of greedy consumerism, and for women this message translates into a pair of shoes for every occasion under the sun.

Women are not the only culprits. Young men, even those whose budgets are severely limited, feel compelled to demonstrate their manliness through the latest pair of Nike sneakers, those worn on their favorite sport's hero. Boys have been known to engage in theft and even warfare in pursuit of Michael Jordan brand-name sneakers.

Shoes are clearly a status symbol which crosses gender lines. When my cousin was six years old, she was in a Puma club: which six year old could possess the most colored Pumas? Whoever could acquire these would be queen for the day. Imagine a world where six year olds must own ten pairs of pink, purple, orange Pumas?

And so we reach the end of the road; we rest our weary feet. In the 21st century we have fallen for all the traps that imprison not just our feet, but our souls: diseased consumerism; sickening status; corrupted competition. This journey begins the moment we say yes to the dream inside the glass window.

Imagine the world with a different set of dreams, one where the manure, the sand, the soil could sink into our toes, saturate our skin. Perhaps we'd be able to experience the earth, as the explorers once did, reeling in the pure joy of discovery.

Author Biographies

Jacqueline Annette is a recent MFA graduate, novelist in progress, and long time performance poet whose other lives include former shoe salesperson, former licensed nurse, intermittent business woman, crafter, jeweler and (currently) adjunct professor at Essex County College in New Jersey. She is the winner of The Meyer Cohn Graduate Award in Literature, as well as the Adria Swartz Award for Woman's Fiction (both in 2011) and has published poems in various literary magazines, some of which appear in her forthcoming collection *Seduction of a Pale Purple Rage*. Some of her experience as a teacher of ESL will be incorporated in a series of connected essays called *Life in Transition*.

Doris Barkin, Ph.D. is a lecturer of English at The City College of New York. She teaches literature and creative writing, and serves as faculty advisor to Promethean. She has served as a contributing editor on various publications, has published in publications such as *American Book Review*, and is currently the judge of various writing awards, including the NYC Poetry Festival. She lives and works in Manhattan.

Gladys E. Perez-Bashier, also known as Poppy, is a founding member of Clique Calm Books Inc./Foundation (an independent multicultural small press, cliquecalm.com) and a performance artist. She was reared in Clinton Hill, Brooklyn and is the author of *Creepin' Through da Hinge*. Additionally, she is also the editor of *HEAL: Between the Pages of These Folks We Seek a Panacea*, a culturally diverse anthology of poems, short stories, chapters of novels, and songs. She is an alumna of The City College of New York's Graduate Creative Writing Program. She is currently teaching in New York City and working on a second novel.

Elana Bell's first collection of poetry, *Eyes, Stones* (2012) was selected as the winner of the 2011 Walt Whitman Award from Academy of American Poets. Her work has recently appeared in *agni, Harvard Review, Massachusetts Review*, and elsewhere. Elana has led creative writing workshops for women in prison, for educators, for high school students in Israel, Palestine and throughout the five boroughs of New York City, as well as for the pioneering peace building and leadership organization, Seeds of Peace, www.elanabell.com

Ourida Chaal was born in France of Algerian descent. She studied Social Sciences at Warwick University and graduated with Honors in 2009. The working mother of two, she writes in her spare time. "I have no real writing credentials, other than writing from my heart and from life experiences of which I am still trying to make sense. Writing has been a positive way of rationalizing the past, and to a greater extent, bringing peace out of chaos." Ourida lives in Coventry, West Midlands (UK)

Victoria A. Chevalier is an Associate Professor of English at Medgar Evers College (CUNY). Her current book manuscript, *Black Things*, argues for a relationship between material cultures and trauma theory in twentieth century American literatures which wrestle with histories of enslavement and colonialism. Her next project will be a comparative study of U.S. Latino and Caribbean literatures. She lives and works in Brooklyn, NY.

Karen Clark (BA in English & German, Barnard; MFA, Creative Writing, CCNY/CUNY [City College of New York and City University of New York]) spent much of her life in the retail book business, and owned a used bookshop in NYC. She has published several poems, and has received awards for short fiction and for excellence in medieval literature. Karen is a contributing editor for the Young Adult anthology My *Best Friend's Secrets: Life on the Moon*. She lives in New York with her husband and her son.

Elayne Clift, a writer, journalist and lecturer, is a Vermont Humanities Council Scholar and columnist for the Keene (NH) *Sentinel* and Brattleboro (VT) *Commons*. Her latest book is *Hester's Daughters*, a novel based on *The Scarlet Letter*. Her website is elayneclift.com.

Lisa S. Coico is the 12th president of The City College of New York and the first City University of New York graduate to lead one of its senior colleges. Dr. Coico is a nationally prominent educator and researcher, and former Provost and Executive Vice President of Academic Affairs and Professor of Surgery at Temple University. Dr. Coico earned a BS with honors in biology from Brooklyn College and she received her doctorate in microbiology and immunology from Weill Cornell Medical College of Cornell University.

Melissa Connelly has published in American Heritage Magazine. She received her MFA from The City College of New York in 2009. Her first novel is called *This Truth, This Hard and Precious Stone*. She lives in Brooklyn with her family, where she is the director of a preschool.

Stephanie Darrow, MA, MFA, is a high school English teacher in New York City. She holds advanced degrees in Adolescent Education and Creative Writing, and her writing has appeared in *Promethean, Poetry in Performance*, and *Stain Anthology*. She co-created, edited and was published in *The Queer Convention Literary Magazine*. She is the 2008 recipient of the Pamela Laskin Award in Children's Writing.

Lyn Di Iorio is the author of the novel *Outside the Bones* (2011), which won ForeWord Review's 2011 Silver Book of the Year Award in the category of literary fiction, was Best Debut Novel on the 2011 Latinidad List, and was a finalist for the John Gardner Fiction Prize, and other prizes. She was also #2 on the 2012 Top Ten Latino Authors to Watch and Read List. A Professor of English at the City College of New York and the Graduate Center of the City University of New York, she is also the author of *Killing Spanish: Literary Essays on Ambivalent U.S. Latino/a Identity* (2004) and the co-editor of *Contemporary U.S. Latino Literary Criticism* (2007) and *Moments of Magical Realism in U.S. Ethnic Literatures* (2012). She received her bachelor's degree from Harvard University, a master's degree from Stanford University's Creative Writing Program, where she was a Patricia Harris fellow, and her Ph.D. from the University of California at Berkeley. She is currently at work on a second novel called *The Sound of Falling Darkness*, an excerpt of which was a runner-up for the 2011 Pirate's Alley Faulkner Society Novel-in-Progress Award.

Lynn Dion, MA, MFA, is an Adjunct Lecturer in both English and Psychology at the City College of New York. She holds advanced degrees in Music, Yiddish Studies, and Psychology as well as the MFA in Creative Writing, and her work has appeared in *The Promethean* and various publications of the YIVO Institute. Two essays and selections from a projected volume of translated essays of the poet and critic Yankev Glatshteyn will appear in spring 2013 issues of *Hektoen International*, Telling Our Stories Press, and *Pakntreger*, the journal of The National Yiddish Book Center, respectively.

Emma Dora Ruth Ziegellaub Eichler graduated summa cum laude from Columbia University with a degree in Computer Science and is now a software engineer at Facebook. She wrote "Our Soles" during her senior year at Stuyvesant High School. Since then, her shoe collection has diversified and now includes heels as well as flats. In addition to writing and shoe-shopping, she enjoys hiking, board games, impressionist art, and novels-especially Jane Austen's Emma, her namesake. She was born and raised in New York City and doesn't plan on moving away any time soon.

Millie Falcaro is a multi-disciplined artist whose poems have appeared in *Chronogram, Avocet, Tapestries, Flesh* and *Darkling*. Her photographs have been exhibited in both solo and group exhibitions, have been published in *Adirondack Review, Avocet* and *Promethean*, and have also appeared in film and television productions and in the movies The "Devil Wears Prada" and "It's Complicated". She directs the Photography Program at Marymount Manhattan College in her native New York City, where she reside with her husband, who is a painter.

N Lynne Fix, MIB, JD, is currently founding a company on Digital Publishing. She has authored books on Chinese Law and Photographic Essays on national development. She has worked as an editor at a small publishing house and as a newsletter editor for the California Writers Club. She is currently publishing two books: *Sinoscapes: Images of a Developing Land* and *Life and Death on a Contested Island*. She lives and blogs in the San Francisco Bay Area.

Mary Frankel, after a satisfying and long career at universities and medical schools, is happily retired and engaged in all manner of interesting volunteer pursuits in the arts and social services. She continues to find that shoes greatly enhance her daily living and wakes up each morning pondering what pair she shall wear today. Shoes are like lovers—a wise woman does not keep count.

Missa Goehring-Plosky writes the popular blog "Missa the Staycation Mama" about the intersection of travel, style, art and parenting in New York City. She works as a freelance writer and business strategy and marketing consultant in addition to full-time motherhood. Missa has a BA in English from the University of Delaware and lives in Manhattan with her husband and two young daughters.

Diane Goettel, a Sarah Lawrence graduate, is the executive editor of Black Lawrence Press.

Margarette Gulinello is an NYPD Sergeant who is currently working on her first novel. She has studied writing at City College and at Sarah Lawrence College, and has recently completed a screenplay, All I Want for Christmas, which she co-authored with Karen Clark. She lives in New York with her husband and son.

Laura Hinton is a Professor of English at the City College of New York, and is the author of a poetry book, *Sisyphus My Love (To Record a Dream in a Bathtub)*, a critical book, *The Perverse Gaze of Sympathy: Sadomasochistic Sentiments from Clarissa to Rescue 911*, and co-editor of *We Who Love to Be Astonished: Experimental Women's Writing and Performance Poetics*. Her essays, poet interviews, reviews, and poems have appeared in numerous journals. Her blog about multi-media poetry Chant de la Sirene can be read at www.chantdelasirene.com.

JP Howard (aka Juliet P. Howard) is a poet, Cave Canem graduate fellow, original member of The Hot Poets Collective and native New Yorker. She co-founded Women Writers in Bloom Poetry Salon and Blog (WWBPS), a forum offering women writers at all levels a venue to come together in a positive and supportive space. WWBPS hosts monthly literary Salons in NY and the blog accepts submissions of poetry.

Mardi Jaskot was born and raised in Hawaii where she often was barefoot. She received her B.A. in Creative Writing from the University of Puget Sound, lived in and around Seattle, and thought she was too cool for Birkenstocks. Currently, she belongs in Brooklyn, where she often wears boots. She recently earned her MFA from The City College of New York, and was awarded the Graduate Award for Children's Literature. Mardi's work has appeared in *Promethean*, *Queer Conventions*, *SynApse*, and *Poetry In Performance*.

Laurel Kallen is a poet and speechwriter who teaches at The City University of New York. She is the recipient of the Stark Short Fiction Award and the Teacher/Writer Award. Her work has appeared in journals, including *La Petite Zine*, *Atlanta Review*, *Big Bridge*, *Portland Review*, *Devil's Lake* and *Amarillo Review*. Laurel is the author of *The Forms of Discomfort*, a collection of poetry by Finishing Line Press.

Maia Wynne Kallen was born and raised in New York City. She received a B.A. in psychology from Boston University, where she also minored in English literature. In addition to writing, Maia has a passion for dancing. She studied classical ballet at the Joffrey Ballet School for two years as a full-time trainee and currently studies ballet, modern, and contemporary techniques at Alvin Ailey. Maia is a writing tutor at the City University of New York.

Kathleen Kesson is a former dancer/choreographer, now Professor of Teaching, Learning and Leadership at Long Island University-Brooklyn, where she teaches courses in the foundations of education and teacher research. She is currently completing a memoir about unschooling her four sons, entitled *Unschooling in Paradise*.

Pamela L. Laskin is a lecturer in the CCNY/CUNY English Department, where she directs the Poetry Outreach Center. Her poetry chapbooks include *Grand Central Station* (Millennium Poetry Prize), *Remembering Fireflies; Secrets of Sheets; Ghosts, Goblins, Gods and Geodes; Van Gogh's Ear; Daring Daughters/Defiant Dreams; The Plagiarist;* and *The*

Bonsai Curator. Her Young Adult novel Visitation Rites was published in 2012. *Homer the Little Stray Cat* is her most recent children's book. A memoir, *My Life in Shoes*, came out in 2011. Many of her short stories have been published, too, including two YA stories, one in *Young Miss* and the other in *Sassy*. She has edited two anthologies: *The Heroic Young Woman* (2006), a book of original feminist fairy tales, and *Life on the Moon: My Best Friend's Secrets*, a collection of young adult fiction.

Tina Lincer, a native of Queens, NY, has chronicled everything from mid-life to the writing life for the *Albany Times Union, Writer's Digest, The Women's Times* and WAMC public radio. Her essays have been featured in many anthologies, including *Words on Ice: A Collection of Hockey Prose*, and four books in the *Cup of Comfort* series. Her work also has been published by *The New York Daily News, The Sun*, the *Los Angeles Times Syndicate* and *The Jewish Monthly*. A senior writer and editor at Union College in upstate New York, she is currently working on a sister-themed memoir and a novel, *The Wife Across the Street*.

Anne Meara (September 20, 1929-May 23, 2015) appeared on Broadway in films and television programs during a career as actress and comedian spanning over fifty years. Author of the comedy *After Play*, she also wrote numerous memoir pieces and comic material. The mother of Amy and Ben Stiller, Anne was married to her comedy partner Jerry Stiller for over sixty years. An Upper West Sider, she resided in New York City.

Gloria Mindock is editor of Červená Barva Press, Istanbul Literary Review, an online journal based in Turkey and one of the USA editors for Levure Littéraire. She is the author *of Blood Soaked Dresses* (2007), *Nothing Divine Here* (2010), and *La Portile Raiului* (2010), translated into the Romanian by Flavia Cosma. Widely published in the USA and abroad, her poetry has been translated and published in Serbian, French, Romanian, and Spanish. Her chapbook, *Pleasure Trout* is forthcoming from Muddy River Press.

Rebecca Minnich grew up in the upper Midwest and has lived in Brooklyn, New York for fifteen years. She has an MFA in creative writing from City College of New York. Her writing has appeared in *POZ, MAMM, Z, Promethean*, and *Construction*, among others. She does not own a single pair of pumps.

Mary Morris is the author of six novels, including *Revenge*, three collections of short stories, and four travel memoirs, including *The River Queen*. Her stories have appeared in such places as *The Atlantic*,

Ploughshares, and *Narrative*. Morris teaches writing at Sarah Lawrence College. For more information see her website. www.marymorris.net.

Maryam Mortaz's first collection of stories, *Pushkin and Other Stories*, was published in Persian, in Iran in 2001. Since moving to the United States and switching to writing in English, her stories have appeared in such magazines as *Bomb, Callaloo, New Review of Literature*, as well as in the collection from the University of Arkansas Press, *Tremors: New Writing from Iranian-American Writers*. She lives in New York City and is a literary translator of Persian and a graduate student in Mental Health Counseling.

Patty Nasey has worked for a variety of publications including Time Out New York, LUCKY, Teen Vogue, JANE, Travel + Leisure, Entertainment Weekly and SPY. Originally from California, she resides in New York City with her husband, two daughters and a dog.

Eden Novak is a musician, actress, monologist and spoken word performer. She is currently completing a Master's Degree in Rehabilitative Counseling at Northeastern IL University. She was a blogger for the Founding Moms and Women's Health Foundation. Her work has been published in *Seeds Journal* and *After Hours, a Journal of Chicago Writing and Art*. She co-wrote and directed, *She Comes Undone: Meditations from Women Mustering the Audacity to Make Themselves Happy*, a multi-media performance. She has studied writing at The Clearing School in Ellison Bay, WI., and Northeastern Illinois University with author Alicia Erian. She lives in the Chicago area with her poet husband.

Carla Porch lives in Southern California, where the temperate climate allows her to wear sandals and boots year-round. In addition to writing and exploring French, she is the CFO of Alex Stark Feng Shui, an architectural consultancy based in Los Angeles. Her essays and critiques have been published in a variety of literary anthologies and journals. Her collection of creative nonfiction, *Union Lake*, was published in 2014.

Diana M. Raab is an award-winning memoirist, poet, essayist, instructor, editor, blogger and author of eight books, including *Regina's Closet, Healing With Words, Listening to Africa, Writers and Their Notebooks*, and *Writers on the Edge*. She teaches journaling and writing for healing across the country. She is widely published in national trade and literary magazines, and is also a regular blogger for *The Huffington Post* at-huffingtonpost.com/Diana-m-raab. Her website is dianaraab.com.

Samantha Reiser was an English Concentrator at Harvard College, where she graduated in 2011, with honors. Her senior thesis was a finalist for The Yale Younger Poetry Award, and several of the poems in her collection have been published in *Lyre, Lyre, J Journal*, and *Poetry in Performance*, among others. Her experience as a teacher in Namibia for World Teach has informed much of her writing, and she continues to write poetry and non-fiction. She worked at Human Rights Watch for several years, and will be attending law school in 2015.

Monica Rose is a writer and educator. She teaches writing to immigrants at the City University of New York, and has taught Mindful Writing classes at the Brooklyn Zen Center. Monica recently completed a memoir, All What it Is. An excerpt from this memoir will be printed in the upcoming issue of Zen Monster Magazine.

Katherine Schifani is a graduate of the U.S. Air Force Academy and spent seven years on active duty in the Air Force. She is pursuing an MFA at Seattle Pacific University and lives in Colorado.

D.L. Stein, a former Wallace Stegner Fellow at Stanford University, has published poetry and prose in many varied reviews, journals, and anthologies. *Alice in Deutschland* (2011) is her latest book of poems.

Vivien (Vicky) Tartter is a Professor of Psychology at City College, and member of the Doctoral faculty of Psychology and of Speech and Hearing Sciences at the Graduate and University Center of CUNY. Her professional specialty is psychology of language and communication. She has two grown sons who have taught her much about enjoying survival in the outdoors and in the rest of life.

Estha Weiner's newest poetry collection is *In the Weather of the World* (2013) She is author of *The Mistress Manuscript* (2009) and *Transfiguration Begins At Home* (2009); and co-editor/contributor to *Blues for Bill: A Tribute to William Matthews* (2005.) Her poems have appeared in numerous anthologies and magazines, including *The New Republic* and *Barrow Street*. Nominated for a 2008 Pushcart Prize, she was a 2005 winner of a Paterson Poetry Prize, and a 2008 Visiting Scholar at The Shakespeare Institute, Stratford, England. Estha is founding director of Sarah Lawrence College NY Alumnae Writers Nights, Marymount Writers Nights, and a Speaker on Shakespeare for The New York Council For The Humanities. She is a Professor in the English Dept. at City College of NY, and serves or has served on the Poetry/Writing faculties of The Frost Place, The Hudson Valley Writers Center, Stonecoast Writers Conference, Poets and Writers, Poets House, and The Writers Voice. She also serves on the Advisory Board of Slapering Hol Press,

Hudson Valley Writers Center. In her previous life, Estha was an actor and worked for BBC Radio.

Suzanne Weyn is a novelist writing for children and young adults. Find her on Wikipedia, also as Suzanne Weyn author on Facebook, or at her website Suzanneweynbooks.com. She is best known for her *Bar Code Tattoo* trilogy, her ecological thriller *Empty* and for her historical sequel to *Frankenstein, Dr. Frankenstein's Daughters.*

Alyssa Yankwitt is an Adjunct Lecturer at City College in the English department, where she also earned her MFA. She is also one of the Instructional Staff Developers for Poetry Outreach, an organization bringing poetry into NYC schools. Her poems have been published in numerous journals, magazines, and anthologies. She lives in Brooklyn, NY, when she is not out wandering the farthest corners of the world.

Dr. Johanna Shira Youner is an active expert spokesperson for the APMA (American Podiatric Medical Association) and an Executive Board member of the New York State Podiatric Medical Association. A board certified foot surgeon, she received her Doctorate of Podiatric Medicine from California College of Podiatric Medicine in 1990 and her BA degree from Barnard College in1983. Having completed three years of residency training in both podiatric medicine and surgery, with experiences that vary from assisting some of New York City's finest plastic surgeons to training at the Leper Colony in Carville, Louisiana, her techniques of foot care continue to be cutting edge. Dr. Youner is very active in the media, writing for magazines that include In Style and Bottom Line Health since 1996. She has been in private practice at 40 Park Avenue in New York City.

CPSIA information can be obtained
at www.ICGtesting.com
Printed in the USA
LVHW082023180619
621611LV00006B/107/P